LOST
IN
CHIAPAS

LOST IN CHIAPAS

by

JOHN SCHERBER

The Fifteenth Book in the Murder
in Mexico Series

San Miguel Allende Books
San Miguel de Allende, Gto, Mexico

ACKNOWLEDGMENTS

Any book starts as an idea, and by its completion becomes a joint effort.

Thanks to all the following:
Lander Rodriguez for the cover design.
Julio Mendez for website design.

To my writer's work group in San Miguel for constant input and critiques: Florence Grende, Christina Johnson, Michael Landfair, Marcia Loy, Dr. Cynthia Miller, and Lynda Schor.

For editing and many valuable suggestions, my wife, Kristine Scherber.

This is a work of fiction. Any resemblance to actual persons, living or dead, is entirely coincidental.

ISBN 978-0-9906551-3-8

San Miguel Allende Books
San Miguel de Allende, GTO, México.

www.sanmiguelallendebooks.com

Also by John Scherber

FICTION

The Devil's Workshop
Eden Lost
The Amarna Heresy
Beyond Terrorism: Survival

NONFICTION

San Miguel de Allende: A Place in the Heart
A Writer's Notebook
Into the Heart of Mexico: Expatriates Find Themselves off the Beaten Path
Living in San Miguel: The Heart of the Matter

For Kristine

CHAPTER ONE
ON THE ROAD AGAIN

Not exactly 221B Baker Street, is it?" The man with one foot on my front step shook my hand too vigorously, chuckling at his own joke, but a trace of nervousness lingered in his voice. At my shoulder, my partner Maya gave me a startled look.

"That would be Sherlock Holmes' digs in London," I said, more to her than our visitors. "Please come in."

"I'm Garrett Anderson and this is my wife, Zina."

He had emailed me five days earlier to ask if they could interview us at the Paul Zacher Agency about a problem they had with their daughter. They didn't give us any more detail than that, even though he'd phoned afterward to confirm our appointment.

My first impression was that his clothes looked as if they'd been purchased especially for this visit to San Miguel de Allende. His pale olive-colored travel shirt was all straps and flapped pockets, nicely ironed and creased, but it didn't look like it had ever seen any road service before. His left hand gripped a hat with the right side brim turned up in a sassy curl like an Australian bush hat. Zina Anderson wore a khaki golf skirt with comfortable walking shoes. With it she had on a golf polo with a light weight navy vest. At least they hadn't showed up in shorts and tank tops, thinking all of México was tropical. We're at 6400 feet here and the climate is all about moderation. The beach is too far away in both directions to be handy on a hot day.

The Andersons' appearance gave me the impression that some upscale outfitter in the States had furnished them with off the rack safari gear, as if their trip could mutate into a trek through the bush at any time without notice. I guess you never know what you're going to discover in the mountains of central México. Zina's makeup was a degree too careful and complete for a Tuesday morning in the second half of November. They both looked like they were a comfortable fifty years old and thought it was their prime.

"I'm Paul Zacher—we spoke on the phone yesterday—and this is Maya Sanchez, my partner and the head of the Zacher Agency." His eyebrows went up as I invited them inside. With a ruddy complexion, Garrett Anderson was about my own height, a fraction over six feet, but he had twenty pounds on me. He had insisted the meeting today would be with the Agency principals only. I merely agreed to that without suggesting to him that we only used principals.

The Andersons looked like prosperous people who were used to being fully in command of their home turf, but today found themselves a bit off their best game on unfamiliar ground. Their balance appeared to be slightly impaired as they stepped into the foyer, watching their footing on the slate tiles. Garrett started eyeing the two Diego Rivera copies I had painted but he didn't ask about them. Zina looked back uncertainly over her shoulder after she crossed the threshold. I checked the street too, but no one was following them. We don't get much trouble here unless we ask for it.

The Agency doesn't have an office for interviews as such, so Maya and I led them into the great room, where they sat on the sofa facing the fireplace. It's more informal and relaxing that way. I think that being inside someone's house makes it also feel more confidential. No one is just going to come walking in as you sit there telling your family secrets. Opposite our guests, over the carved stone mantle, Maya stared back at us out of my painting of her dressed as Frida Kahlo. Zina looked around the room as if assessing our design taste or our furnishings budget. Both could vary widely.

"I believe you're looking for your daughter," Maya said, "is that right? Please start by telling us about her." Many times clients don't know where to begin. For this meeting Maya had put on a pair of black slacks and a white silk blouse. At five-foot-six with a trim build, it was a good choice for her business look.

They both nodded gravely, glanced at each other with raised eyebrows for a cue, and Garrett Anderson began.

"Our daughter's name is Megan Anderson and she's twenty-four years old. Until she finished college last spring, she had spent her entire life in Minnesota, except for a two-month-long summer break in Spain two years ago."

His eyes flickered up and down between the portrait of Maya and then Maya herself. "When she graduated from the University of Minnesota five months ago she wasn't sure what to do next."

"Her degree is in anthropology," Zina added, parenthetically, with a slightly perplexed shake of the head. "She likes to study primitive societies and how they work."

The clear subtext was that Megan had not grown up in one and might have to go farther afield to see one in action.

I didn't ask whether in Zina Anderson's mind today's México might fit that description. Some days it certainly did. Stands selling cow's head tacos came readily to mind. Still, you never know how Americans view this country, and I'd be the first to admit that in some places here it's still only 1950 on a good day. We don't mind that. I'd rather have it be that way than chasing the latest trend all the time.

At the mention of anthropology, Garrett's left hand twitched with a gesture that may have been more dismissive. "Let's just say that after graduation Megan found herself at loose ends. I mean, is there any clear job pathway with a degree like that? Even with good grades, and she had plenty of them, it's still a dead end. She couldn't even teach without going on to get a master's degree at least."

"Oh, Garry, you have to give her *some* credit, even if that wasn't the major you would've chosen for her. She did minor in Spanish, don't forget that part," said Zina. "Surely that's worth something."

"Right. That's going to be a big help when she ends up chopping lettuce at Taco Bell. Anyway, right before she graduated she got connected somehow to an organization that sends missionaries down here to Chiapas. I'm not sure how she met them. I only know she sure as hell didn't get that idea from either of us."

"We're Unitarians ourselves," said Zina, with a complacently tolerant smile, "so, as you can see…"

"What you can see is that we don't entertain a lot of mumbo-jumbo at our services, right? Quite frankly, I thought that was a bunch of shameless zealots she'd gotten herself hooked up with. But that's just me."

Searching for something more interesting to look at, he waved his own comment aside, and ended up staring at Maya. She smiled at him as if he were the first man who'd ever noticed her, although she had minored with honors in flirting, and had even caused talk of starting a new major in that field, something many Mexican women would've flocked to in droves.

Zina Anderson made a vague gesture, as if the word *zealot* was one that rarely surfaced in either her vocabulary or among her lunch companions. "But let me finish, Garry! She brought two of them over to the house one night during her last term of school, kids wearing khaki pants and starched button-down shirts on a hot day in May. It seems like we never have any spring in Minnesota anymore. They wouldn't even have a glass of wine with us, like they thought it was a sin or something. I mean, I even offered them a dry white." Zina sighed softly. "Well, Megan wanted to be involved somehow, and when no promising job offers came her way, I think she started looking farther afield, in her mind, I mean. I could see that happening."

"Too damn far afield, if you ask me." Garrett shook his head. "I always thought she would've done better with a marketing major. A lot of people noticed that she had a kind of magnetism about her that would've been an asset in that field."

Zina looked at him briefly and then back at us.

"She doesn't strictly have to work, you know, because she has a small trust fund from her grandfather's estate." She spoke in an offhand manner, as if this were nothing unusual.

"How much does that bring in?" asked Maya.

"It pays her around $4,000 a month. But it's not an interest payment, because it's an income stream from a small company her grandfather started that the family still owns and operates."

"That's good because there's no capital she can get at," Garrett added. "It's all locked up in a trust."

Thinking this was not the best of terms for it, in my mental notes I wrote down, *absence of trust, possibly on both sides?* "That would provide her a very comfortable life down here. And where do you live?" A monthly check like that would also appeal strongly to a cult leader recruiting new members.

"Edina," Zina said. "That's a southwestern suburb of Minneapolis. First tier."

"I've been there," I said quietly, not expecting to hear this. "It was on our first case, the murder of Toby Cross. His family lived there then and we went back for the funeral."

"In the winter," said Maya, shaking her head dubiously. "It was very sad. We didn't know how they could bury him, with the ground all frozen so hard like stone. Imagine."

"I can recall that we heard about it at the time," said Zina, "partly because it happened in México, which as we all know from the news, can be so dangerous, although we don't know the Crosses socially. They live in the Country Club neighborhood and we're in Indian Hills, on Navajo Trail. It's much woodsier there, of course," she said with a wrinkle of her nose.

"And how did that case come out for you?" said Garrett, with an air of throwing out a tough question.

"We solved it, and the murderer was apprehended." I didn't look at Maya as I said this. She had, in fact, killed the murderer of Toby Cross herself, and that finished the case.

"So what would you like the Paul Zacher Agency to do for you?" Maya said after a moment of silence in which the Andersons exchanged glances.

"We would like you to find Meg and bring her home," said Zina. "Or at least, watch her get on a nonstop plane to Minneapolis where we could meet her at the other end. As I said, part of our concern is that it's so dangerous down here."

I had heard about the danger of México so many times that I'd long ago stopped trying to rebut statements like that. Next we'll be seeing folks coming down here wearing Kevlar vests for underwear.

"We've already been in contact with the police and both the hospitals down there in Chiapas," said Garrett. "They had no information for us."

"It sounds like you think she's been brainwashed," Maya said. "Is that true?"

"I don't know what else to think," said Garrett, rubbing his palms together. "She's always been a sensible girl, and a strong one, I used to think, goin' her own way, but these people she got in with, I just don't know how it could've happened. Maybe they've got her hooked on drugs. This is México, you know."

Maya nodded slowly. "I've noticed that too."

"She might not be as tough as you think, Garry. She likes to put on a good front, but inside, I don't know. Sometimes I wonder if she isn't just still a kid at heart, dressing up to make herself look like a grown up." She turned to Maya. "Megan was always into costumes, you know? Halloween was her favorite time of the year. Remember that one when she was a witch in a miniskirt, Garry?" He ignored this as if he did.

A barrage of explosives went off in the street outside, coming at us like mortar rounds. Zina and Garrett both sprang to their feet, although she didn't fall into his arms. I got up and put a steady hand on both their shoulders.

"Don't worry! Please! It's Revolution Day, November 20. Fireworks are traditional." Perplexed, they only looked at each other.

"You mean it's not an attack?" Zina said.

"You mean they *celebrate* revolution here?" said Garrett at the same moment.

I nodded solemnly. What did he think the fireworks on the Fourth of July celebrated? I brought them both a glass of cold water while Maya got them seated again.

"What if we find Megan and she won't come back with us?" I said, after a long silence while they readjusted their composure.

"Why on earth wouldn't she?" Anderson gave me a blank look as if this were beyond possibility. "How could she resist being rescued from a mistake like that? Surely she's had enough time to realize it by now."

"You said she was twenty-four. She might have developed a mind of her own since she left home," said Maya. "It would be the time for that to happen with many women of her age. Maybe that's even *why* she left home."

Garrett shook his head as if this idea was well beyond him, and not in a direction he was headed in.

"I have to tell you," I said, "that this would be a long distance field investigation with a lot of time and expenses, but I'm sure you've already thought of that. Chiapas is not an hour's drive away. It's on the Guatemala border, so it's far south of here, in fact it's the southernmost part of México, even below the Yucatán, and somewhat to the east."

"We do know she was in San Cristobal de la Something, for a while at first. I could find it on the map, if you've got one."

"Right," I said, "it's San Cristobal de las Casas. A lot of the area around that city is Zapatista country, so it's semi-independent. That means when you get out of town, there are no federal or state police, no government health care or education."

"So what you're sayin' is that it's a wide open town." Garrett gave us an uncomfortable look.

"I don't know how wide open the city itself is. It has the reputation of being a refined place, but I'm just telling you what I've read about the broader area, and by that I mean Chiapas as a state. I haven't been down there myself, but I know it's very rugged country. What do you have as her last address?"

"We can give you what we were using to communicate with her," said Garrett, "but she stopped emailing us three months ago, not even responding to ours, and her cell phone doesn't work any more."

"Has she been silent for that length of time in the past?" Maya said. "I suppose she hasn't ever been away from home that long."

"Well, here's what it is. She's been angry with Garry a couple of times before when she wouldn't talk to him for a while, like several weeks. We weren't sure that this silence wasn't another period like that." From an inner pocket of her vest Zina Anderson produced a folded sheet of paper that listed all the information they had on Megan's circumstances in Chiapas.

The top of the page displayed three photos of her from different angles. She looked like an appealing young woman with an oval face, clear features and thick blond hair hanging straight down from a part in the center. Her lips were full and sensuous, her nose straight, and her look was direct and unwavering. Based on her appearance, she did not resemble a mental drifter, unable to decide what she wanted to do or how to go about it. Nor did she seem like she'd be open to the oppressive and controlling dictates a cult leader might impose on her. Of course, the Andersons had not used that word, but it was already in the air.

I wondered for a moment whether her parents had read her right. Sometimes adults watch their children get older year by year without seeing them change into grownups. They remain Little Timmy or Tammy, always in need of protection and counsel. Garrett Anderson looked like he had some experience in his life of events not going exactly his way. How he dealt with it was another question that couldn't be answered this early in a case, but that didn't mean we wouldn't eventually find out.

"Do you have any specific reason to think she might be in danger?" I said.

"Nothing concrete, but we are worried." Zina's two-handed grip tightened on her purse.

"Was there anything alarming in her emails, before she stopped writing back? Anything that to you suggested a threat?" Maya said.

Zina shook her head. "Nothing much. The tone didn't ever change."

"Did she mention any of her friends down there by name?" I said.

"One of those button down missionary boys she went with was named Leo Cochrane. We knew that before she left. Other than that, once she got there we saw hardly any detail in what she wrote; it was more like she was simply staying in touch. But she is that way sometimes; Meg doesn't always want to share what's going on in her life. I was private like that myself at her age, but then, my father was a tyrant."

"What she was sending felt like no more than a damned courtesy to me," said Garrett.

"Can I ask why you chose the Zacher Agency?" Maya said.

"Sure, that was easy enough." He smiled broadly. "You're the only American-style detective agency operating in México that I could find, and we don't speak any Spanish. Even after a long search by my attorney, we couldn't come up with anybody else, other than some agency at Lake Chapala that was more about real estate and title issues. I'll be copying him on everything you send us, by the way."

"Then it wasn't because of our shining reputation," I said, nonetheless grateful for this lukewarm vote of confidence.

"No. But we would like to have a few references, if you don't mind."

We discussed terms for a while. This was Maya's area, and she spelled it out by cost per hour of time spent traveling, a different and higher rate for hours spent in investigation, the fact that we don't mark up our expenses and we always submit receipts, and that there would be three of us on the ground in Chiapas. I didn't say this was because it would be riskier than Puerto Vallarta or Edina, Minnesota, but that's what I was thinking.

We talked about our reporting procedures. Maya then outlined our different areas of expertise, starting with Cody and his background as a Peoria homicide detective for thirty years. She addressed his ability, at 230 pounds and six-foot-three in height, to provide muscle on short notice. He had not been able to attend this meeting. When she said I was also a painter, their eyebrows went up, but they didn't comment. Where we left it was that by midafternoon we would email the Andersons copies of three different references, and they would wire $8,000 U.S. as a retainer into our local bank account by the end of business on the day after tomorrow if they wished to proceed. This would cover travel expenses to San Cristobal de las Casas, hotels, meals and a certain amount of time on the ground there. I had instantly realized we wouldn't be flying because we couldn't bring our guns on board. It would be two long days on the road.

Garrett Anderson nodded throughout this explanation. The business part of the investigation appeared to be reassuring in its resemblance to his home turf, and money was not an issue. I hadn't asked what his business was, but he had the manner of someone who was clearly in business for himself, and that, in the end, was where our common ground emerged.

Just before noon, Maya and I stood in the doorway and watched the Andersons walk down Calle Quebrada in the direction of the overpass, a little more than a block away. There they could descend the steps, land on Canal, and easily find a taxi back to their hotel. They'd mentioned they were staying at the Rosewood, an upscale hostelry between the Ancha de San Antonio and Parque Juarez that had figured prominently in an earlier case, one we filed as *The Book Doctor.* Zina Anderson was gripping her husband's arm firmly, as if that were her custom, or it just may have been the irregular sidewalk. They were chatting with a lot of animation, a sign I took to mean that they had found a reason to be confident in the Paul Zacher Agency after all.

Our task was now to find our own reasons to be

as hopeful as the Andersons seemed to be. When we went back inside I called Cody to see if he was back home. I knew that football broadcasts had not yet begun for the day. Even though this was a Tuesday, there must be one happening somewhere.

Late that afternoon an email came in from the Andersons approving our references, and with a brief introduction saying they had attached a string of twenty-two of Megan's emails that were complete up to the start of her silence. The most recent was ninety-three days old. I scanned them briefly and even though I saw some place references I didn't recognize, they seemed routine and as they'd been described. Maya printed them out thinking to go over them with Cody when he came over for a briefing. Ten minutes later a messenger arrived from the Rosewood Hotel. He handed Maya a large envelope containing a sealed letter bearing the name of Megan Anderson and the instructions to hand it to her face to face once we found her. Maya thought there could be no clearer sign of the Andersons' confidence.

"I've got a good feeling about this one," she said, taking my hand. I squeezed it back, although I rarely have a good feeling going into a case. I always feel better when they're finished.

She was more upbeat about this case than most others recently because, she added, it looked like a simple missing persons affair. None of us had ever been to Chiapas, and this was a good excuse to go. It was possible that Megan had zoned out on drugs, I also suggested, and she only needed to be brought out of her fog and packed up for a return flight. That would explain the communications shutdown most easily.

"Probably no one will even be killed," Maya suggested, cheerfully. This was always her hope. I had no response to that. By early evening Cody called back to say he was fully aboard and ready to leave as soon as the deposit hit our account.

On Thursday the $8,000 bank transfer arrived. Maya and I pulled out the suitcases from the storage wall in the art studio. We were feeling good, ready for a break out of town. We had deep pockets behind us, the insights from fourteen earlier cases with widely varied configurations, and nothing to distract us. We all knew that missing person cases tended to be about misunderstandings, about rebellious children or restless spouses nursing an itch for something new. About people whose identity no longer suited them and they were searching for a change of name and scene. It looked like Megan Anderson had not been dragged kicking and screaming into the wilds of southern México; she was a sensible girl who had gone down there herself in the company of Leo Cochrane and simply drifted out of touch. It might even be that she'd ended up in a place with poor Internet service, something we experienced ourselves now and then even

in our house on Quebrada. And Chiapas was not considered to be the model for cutting edge infrastructure
in México.

Like Maya, I also wanted to think we had caught
a break. After all, whatever could go wrong on a simple
case like that?

CHAPTER TWO

On the following Saturday, at the end of the first long day of the trip, we left the toll road (*cuota*) at Oaxaca. It's a lively town where politics is a subject never far from people's minds, as we'd discovered on an earlier case there we filed as *Strike Zone*, but we didn't care to linger. Unofficial roadblocks happen too often in this part of México, and in nearby Michoacán the student teachers love to shut down traffic and steal buses. You never knew when that urge could spread to nearby states, and the most radical groups in Oaxaca were also the teachers and their union. We could always stop for a visit on our return trip, when nothing clouded the horizon ahead of us.

We spent that first night in an old-fashioned eight-room hotel on the southern edge of the city not far from the airport. It was called La Serpiente Emplumada, the Plumed Serpent. This may have been a reference to D. H. Lawrence's novel, but more probably just a local use of part of the national symbolism of México.

The final leg of the trip awaited us in the morning. It was a distinct plus that the high-speed toll road to San Cristobal had recently been completed. I thought the tolls were fairly expensive, but Garrett Anderson had deeper pockets than we did.

Under a dozen flowering trees of a variety I didn't recognize, we gathered in the courtyard of this old converted house that would've been out in the country when it was built. We needed a drink and some light dinner. Only one other table was occupied. It was a romantic young couple in the far corner, and they wouldn't be able to hear us. A cordial host came out to greet us and take our orders. He introduced himself as Plutarco Gomez. All his family welcomed us to Oaxaca, he said, when I told him we were traveling from Guanajuato to Chiapas. Maya took this as a good omen.

"What do we do if this young woman needs a deprogrammer?" Cody asked. "I don't think we can kidnap her outright. I have done that in the past, but it's frowned upon this time, since she's no longer a minor." We needed to rough out a plan, even with the little information we had.

"Well, we've done some other strange things," Maya said, sipping her Chilean cabernet. She had pulled her shoulder-length hair back and tied it loosely with a violet ribbon. Traveling like this, she hadn't put on any makeup, and having just turned thirty, she rarely used much anyway. She always turned heads when she walked down the street, and in our division of tasks, she was always our front line negotiator, whenever it came to that.

"You're the one with a psychology background," I said to Cody. "Couldn't you bring her around yourself? At least enough to get her in shape to travel?"

He made a dismissive gesture with his right hand. "That was a long time ago, and clinical therapy was never my focus in grad school. If that's her problem, the only way we could get her out of there would be to sedate her and stay with her on the plane back to Minneapolis. Help her hold her head up, that kind of thing. We could say she'd had too many cocktails in the airport bar when the plane was late taking off."

"She might be a white knuckle flyer, anyway," I said. "We could also say she's got a delicate stomach and likes to sedate herself a little before she travels."

Maya's extended hands, making a gesture of flat and irrevocable refusal as they slashed outward over the table, nearly knocked all the drinks over. "Look at the calendar. There is *no* way we are going to Minneapolis in the winter again. And it would be me, by the way, and not you guys on the plane with the sedated Miss Megan Anderson, if we found her, because who else is going to get her back into the bathroom and then pull her jeans back up when she can't stand up herself without help?"

"I'm sure that's true, but neither is it part of our

agreement, is it?" I added, always the cool moderate, a position that rarely makes any friends. "There are probably agencies here that could supply a travel companion like you might need for an elderly person who has physical or mental issues."

"Then your task will be to find one of those agencies on short notice in Chiapas," said Maya, finishing her wine with a flourish and summoning the waiter for another with her free hand.

Cody said nothing, but Maya was right. This was not a psychology problem. The case was about reestablishing a family link that had been broken by forces unknown, some of which might be totally benign. Where the Andersons of Edina, Minnesota went from there, once they were all back at home with their storm windows on and the snowplow service scraping their driveway outside, was their own problem. If Megan had found the Unitarian doctrine too diluted to inflame her youthful religious passions, they could sort that out among themselves, on their own time. My recollection from our previous visit that far north was that the state of Minnesota had agencies to deal with everything, issues that people in México could not even imagine. Frostbite, for example. Failing to wear a motorcycle helmet. Here, one helmet, if that many, is shared when three people ride a motorcycle.

The next day, another long one, was mostly a

process of swinging southwest toward the Pacific, but never quite getting there before we turned inland and began the eastward climb toward San Cristobal de las Casas. A year ago, when a long stretch of this freeway was not yet completed, it would have been a different drive entirely. For the last 200 kilometers or so the terrain around us evolved from mixed hardwood and softwood forest to long-needle pines. As we climbed, clouds draped the hillsides and the moister air also felt thinner. We didn't pay much attention to Tuxtla Gutierrez, the state capital; home of the airport that armed travelers couldn't use, and we came to earth an hour and a half afterward in San Cristobal. We had alternated driving, but we were still all ready to settle in.

We pulled up at the Hotel Misión on a busy street. At the edge of *centro*, but not fully part of it, the hotel offered a good-size restaurant that was three-quarters full, so we took that as a positive sign and booked two rooms. It was the kind of place that could suit a busload of tourists, a small business gathering, or a weary detective agency crew a long way from home and more than ready to be finished for the day.

CHAPTER THREE

In the morning, rested, showered, and ready to work, we strolled down to Real de Guadalupe, a pedestrian street that branches off from the large plaza fronting the cathedral. The street was lined with mainly one and two-story façades that housed restaurants, clothing boutiques, galleries, and a surprising number of jewelry shops featuring amber. We settled in at an outdoor coffee bar called Café Opera and ordered breakfast. Wisps of morning fog curled down off the mountains, but the sky was clear in other places over the valley. We had heard San Cristobal was a town with indecisive weather and a lifestyle that drew Europeans in greater numbers than Americans or Canadians. Maybe they thought it felt familiar and alpine.

The foot traffic was still thin that time of the morning, but after we were served, a man my age came through, glanced at an empty table, then paused passing ours. He was average height with thin ginger hair that lifted in subtle waves across his head. His blue eyes crinkled with an easy laugh. "You folks passing through or do you mean to stay a while?"

"Depends," said Cody, with a broad gesture. "Have a seat and talk to us. Maybe you can help us decide. Can we buy you a cup of coffee?"

He said his name was Ian and he'd lived in San Cristobal for seven years.

"Cool mornings here," I said, pointing to his plaid wool jacket as he pulled up a chair. It was fully buttoned up except for the collar.

He shrugged. "But don't worry, it'll come around just fine by lunchtime. I always wear a short-sleeved shirt under this jacket."

"I would've thought you could throw a stone on the Guatemala jungle from here," I said.

"You almost can, but that's at a much lower altitude. We're at 7,000 feet here."

"Do you have much of an expat community?"

"Sure. There are the Warrens, Bill and Naomi, and then Phil Streeter, he's a painter, and me, of course, and Jackie Kassenbaum is a weaver. She shows her stuff up in Oaxaca. Then there are about ten others that come and go. Mostly they come. This is a sweet place."

I was comparing this with the eight to ten thousand expats in San Miguel.

"We have a friend who came down here for a while," said Maya, after a server arrived with Ian's coffee. "I said we'd look her up when we got to San Cristobal. I wonder if you ever ran into her?" She pulled a photo of Megan Anderson out of her shirt pocket and slid it across the table. We had clipped away the contact information and blown up the best of three portrait shots before we left home. That way it didn't look like she was wanted by the law.

Ian squinted at it for a moment. "I think so, although I believe she moved on a few months back. At least I haven't seen her lately. Was she called Meg?"

"Right. She was traveling with a buttoned down guy named Leo, and she may have been trying to hook up with a religious group," I said. "This was the first town she looked at."

"Well, I don't see a lot of that here in San Cris, but there are some Mormon missionaries up in Chamula, which is not that far away in the hills, maybe ten kilometers."

"I don't think the Mormons would be a good fit for her," said Cody.

"It's been kind of rough up there lately anyway. Two guys were caught stealing cars and they were burned alive by the locals."

Maya gave him a blank look. I was recalling the Andersons' question about this being a lawless town. Mainly just outside of it, we had said.

"Then how about Seventh Day Adventist?"

"No," said Cody, with no detail. "Is there anything happening that's centered around a strong charismatic personality, maybe not a conventional sect but more like…"

"A cult?" Ian's forehead wrinkled. His coffee cup paused halfway to his lips.

Unintentionally we all nodded.

He set the cup back down. "Well, I ran into a couple last week that was headed up to Mazintla. They said there's a new group like that up there."

"What's the leader like?" I said. "A guru type? A forceful personality?"

"No. Matter of fact, I heard it was a *bruja*, a witch." He smiled as if this were nothing unusual.

Maya studied his face for a moment. "A witch? A real *bruja*, or just a spiritual leader that was a woman?"

"I couldn't tell you that. This couple seemed kind of sad. I think they'd been up in Baja for a while and run out of money there. Things are cheaper down here away from the beaches. I've got an apartment with its own garden on the edge of centro and it only costs me about $250 a month U.S. But if you can't even manage that, then a cult might be the place to go for group living if you can handle the message that comes with it."

"Where's Mazintla?" I said.

"It's up in the hills above Ocosingo, but it's a tough town to find, I understand. Once you get off the main highway, the roads aren't always passable. That's true of a lot of places up here, though. You're definitely out in the sticks, like we used to say back home."

"But I'm sure there's bus service into a place like that, right?" Cody asked.

Ian laughed. "This is Chiapas, man. Buses need highways. That's fine for the major destinations, but back in the hills like that, deep into Zapatista country, the autonomous zones as they call 'em, then you're all on your own. You won't find any state schools or health care up there, either. After the fighting started twenty years ago, the government walked away from those people, just wrote 'em all off. It was that or exterminate 'em, and that was too hard to justify."

"Is it really dangerous up there? I mean, with the Zapatistas…" asked Maya, an artificially casual tone in her voice. She stirred her coffee, which was now cold, not looking at Ian.

"Some people think so, but I don't. Those are mostly good people who've gotten the short end of the stick and they got damn sick of it."

"So you go up that way yourself now and then?" I said, thinking we'd be needing a guide to find Megan.

"No."

A small group of warmly dressed tourists walked past with two couples arguing in German. The one in the lead was studying a map.

"Was Meg close to anyone here?" said Cody. "Someone she might've told where she was headed?"

Ian thought for a while. "You could ask over at The Scholar. That's a coffee shop and breakfast place on the next street over and down about a block. She and the guy she was with used to hang out with some people over there. Her Spanish was really quite good, better than mine. That's about all I can tell you. Hope you can find her before she gets into any trouble. A lot of people come down here who don't know what they're looking at."

As we left I wondered whether that included us.

At the Scholar we had our second cup of coffee that morning, and it was better than the first. A fireplace opposite our table was crackling with pine logs. The generous brownies were freshly out of the oven and we had three of those too, on Garrett Anderson's dime. The place was filled with expertly handmade furniture. Even the chairs were perfectly designed for comfort, which always says to me that the cabinetmaker knew what he was doing. Putting myself through college I'd been a part-time woodworker, and I know you cannot fake a comfortable chair. And they never happen by accident. The weavings hanging on the walls were crisply made and finely detailed. The color design favored a range of red tones from pink through deep magenta, often with pale green accents. I could see how Megan might have enjoyed hanging out at the Scholar; the whole place felt like a welcome.

In the rear of the room an annex with dimmer lighting displayed two walls of wine bottles from local vintners along with honey and coffee from the area. What I had expected would be a primitive place displayed a consistent sense of upscale design.

The young woman who served us was almost elegant in a straight black skirt with a matching corduroy vest over a crisp white shirt. Her accent was British. "Megan Anderson?" She said as she set down the tray of brownies. "Blond gal, right? American accent like yours? Earnest look to her? Rather a seeker, I should think. This place pulls those in too."

Maya showed her the photo.

"Sure, that'd be the one. But she's gone on, now, don't you know, about three months back or so. She was looking for the real deal. This place was too civilized for her, too polished, I suspect, with so many Brits and Continentals coming through. Not so many Yanks as in the other parts of México."

"What do you mean?" said Cody. "Does Megan have some rough edges?"

"No, not that one, not herself. She didn't mind them on other people, though. She never put on any airs. The times she was in here I thought she was looking for something more intense."

"Like what?" said Maya.

The woman put her pencil to her lower lip. "I'm not really certain, but probably not something you'd find at this altitude."

"Too high?" I said.

"No, too low. I thought she had a spiritual side to her. Just a guess, but there was something about her that was hard to put a name to."

"Are you hinting she was interested in drugs?" Cody said.

"I didn't say that. A lot of things in México will get you off."

"Did she ever say anything about going on to Mazintla?"

She stared at Cody for a moment. "Now that you mention that, I believe she did once or twice. I can't imagine why, though. It's only the dark pine forest up there, and it's about fifteen hundred feet higher than we are here. She'd be in the mist and the wind. Maybe that might be what would suit her."

"What do you mean?" I said.

"I wouldn't take her at face value, I guess is what I'm saying. She looks like she's open like an American pie, you know? But then there's more you don't see for a while. Maybe never."

"What was the guy like that she was with?" Maya said.

"Leonard, was he?"

41

"Leo."

"Right. I didn't fancy him much. Being with her, he was out of his depth, if you ask me."

"But how would they get to Mazintla? We heard there were no buses."

The server smiled like an insider. "Well, what you do around here is find someone who's going in that direction and hitch a ride. Things are more informal in that way than you might be accustomed to. People depend more on themselves." When we all looked at her blankly, she went on. "I would try Artemio Díaz. He goes out that way regularly with medical help for isolated areas, and if he isn't going soon, he might be able to tell you who is. He lives in the street that runs behind the cathedral. It's the blue house without a number."

"I'll go talk to him," said Cody, after she moved on to the next table. "No sense ganging up on the man. I'll get him to agree to take me and then I'll tell him there are three of us."

CHAPTER FOUR
CODY WILLIAMS

"You didn't start out this way," Cody said, leaning back on a creaky wicker chair and crossing his legs in the well-worn stone-paved courtyard. It was about three hours later and he had found the blue house with no problem on a long street that featured façades in reds and ochers. What he wanted next was some idea of Artemio Díaz' credentials, so Cody went on.

"I don't imagine that you planned to do this as your career." The caged gray parrot next to him watched his gestures warily, ready to squawk and flutter at any swift movement. In the entry hallway behind him Cody had seen a low table piled with medical supplies when he came in, as if people dropped things off in passing. He had noticed bandages, disinfectants, and a variety of other items he didn't recognize.

"No, when I started out I never meant to go in this direction." Artemio Díaz shifted in his chair and swirled the glass in his hand.

"But you *are* a doctor? You do have the medical degree. The people who told me about you were a bit vague on detail."

"The credential? Sure, the best. I went to Autonomous University in the capital, and that's where my practice was too, in Colonia Condesa, for many years. I studied in the States for a year too."

"Condesa's a prosperous part of town."

"Sure, for making a great living, but I spent too many years in that neighborhood, as I now realize. I could've spent it better, you know? Rather than making the rich look younger and richer all the time." From the fact that Díaz said this in nearly perfect English, Cody thought he might have had his share of American patients too. Medical tourists, they were called. He'd seen them in San Miguel as well, mostly coming there for plastic surgery or dental work.

"What did you do?"

Díaz smiled. "I was a plastic surgeon, as you would call it. I thought of myself as an artist of lift. I could raise eyelids, butts, boobs, anything that sagged. It was like being in the space program up in Houston; my enemy was gravity in all its manifestations. The game was to defeat it but leave no trace of the battle." His left arm swept the scene as if clearing it of droopy features, and Díaz finished by laughing humorlessly as he pointed at Cody's chin. "For example, now, those jowls you've got there? They're wearing out your collar. I could have them gone in a heartbeat. Take ten years off your age in two hours. Nobody would ever see the scar under your jaw."

Cody had just turned sixty-three. "No thanks. I already figured out how to shave around 'em." Still tough and vigorous, he felt he had earned his rugged looks and he didn't care to give them up.

Díaz' travel pants were heavily worn and stained but still looked like they were clean after many washings. His blue and white plaid shirt would've been a poor choice for the jungle. The do rag on his head, with a tiny knot at the back, could have been found as easily on the dreadlocks of some rapper on the streets of Detroit or South Side Chicago. The doctor took a long pull at his drink and tossed in three more ice cubes from the covered ceramic bucket at his side, using his fingers rather than tongs. He splashed in another round of vodka, not a lot, but more than a taste.

"You sure you won't have a drink? I've got some English gin too, back in the kitchen. It's Gilbey's, I think. I don't use it anymore, myself."

Cody shook his head. It was only two o'clock in the afternoon, and anyway, he preferred rum.

Díaz was an inch less than six feet tall, spare with pale skin, although a rosy flush bloomed on the bridge of his nose and upper cheeks. His gray hair stopped at his collar, cut off squarely by an amateur. His tapering nose was long and thin, and his thick lower lip had been split at the center at some point, but had healed long ago, leaving a pale vertical scar. Díaz' legs might have been slightly too long for his height: a dancer's legs, lean and gangly, ready to move on no notice. Cody thought the doctor was over seventy, but had not found any reason to slow down.

"Your career had a course correction."

"Yes, you could say that. It happened seventeen years ago. Too late perhaps to make a big difference for me, but that was not the case for many others."

Cody tried to put himself in this position, where after a successful career in medicine (or law enforcement, as in his own case), he'd find himself making a sudden left turn. Perhaps he had made a switch like that in joining the Zacher Agency, where strict adherence to the law was never the first priority. It was often mislaid in the pursuit of their own idea of justice, or however close they could get to it. In Cody's experience justice was never more than an approximation whether inside or outside the law. One of the trees dripped on him and he shifted his chair a foot or so, rubbing the damp spot on his thigh. The parrot responded with a blunt uncivil comment and moved further down along his wooden perch, shaking his head.

"Where were you from originally?"

"The state of Coahuila, from a ranching family not far from the border. That's how I could afford medical school. How about you? You seem to be looking for something down here. Maybe you're an archaeologist? There's no shortage of ruins, many of them untouched back in the bush. You could still make a name for yourself in this part of México if you had some backing behind you. Out in the autonomous zones you wouldn't even need a license if you got friendly enough with the locals. They'd all be looking for some shovel work, of course. Naturally you'd keep your political views to yourself, whatever they were."

Cody shook his head. "I've been retired for eight years. Now I'm just a traveler looking for interesting people and places. I happen to like México so I settled here."

"Still, I can see you haven't spent much time in the jungle. Your clothes show hardly any wear. Your skin says you stay out of the sun most of the time. Your fingernails are clean and well trimmed. If I were to speculate a bit, I would guess that your ankles don't show any snakebite scars, either. Shall I go on? You don't need to show me."

"No, but I see your point. I do usually spend more time in the north, that much is true," Cody said uncomfortably, thinking that Díaz knew what he was looking at. He'd only worn these travel clothes for a few days in the Yucatán during the *Predator* investigation, and he never wore them when he was only hanging out around the house. Putting them on this time had made him feel like he was again preparing for something he didn't want to do.

"So what are you searching for here, so far off the beaten path? No one comes to San Cris by accident. This road doesn't go anywhere else. Superficially, the jungle looks much the same everywhere, to those who don't know it. It's the detail that always tells the story, don't you think? What's yours?"

Here Cody felt he was losing this game of bluff, so it was time to ratchet it up a notch.

"Frankly, I'm interested in religion, in all its twists and turns." He didn't hold Díaz' gaze as he said this.

"Hallelujah. When I hear that word, I always suspect I'm being lied to. Why is that?"

"I'm sure it's because you must be, but I'm not a priest."

"Yet, here we sit in the center of eternal religion. In five hundred years the Spanish Catholics have barely dislodged the belief system of the mountain Maya, and in some places, like up in Chamula or Zinacantán, the regular clergy has been expelled from their own churches. So what kind of belief do you favor? Don't tell me you're here to promote Lutheranism or Japanese Shinto."

Cody laughed. "Although I'm not a promoter of anything, I do like the newer religions, and the people who can make one up. The phenomenon of belief right out of the box, where someone can bring in strange ideas and sell them with what looks like divine endorsement. I see the Mormons and other evangelical sects coming down here to market their goods. Being from the nineteenth century, they're far newer than what's already established here, but maybe they're not new enough. What if I had something really new? What if religion has its own fashion cycle, and I had hitched a ride on the newest fad? Could I make some impact here? Could I draw the local people into it?"

"That would depend on what you offered. Like everything else, religion needs a hook. Would it be a new deity you'd be introducing?"

"I'm not sure. Maybe just a new focus, or a new angle of approach. I might have come up with a new way of praying that's better than yours."

Díaz laughed coarsely. "I'm sure that any new one would be. Praying has never gotten me very far in my field. My job is more about maintenance than miracles."

Cody scratched his cheek for a moment. "Do you ever come across any cults on your travels?"

"Everywhere," said Díaz, shaking his head. "This place was built on cults. Some of them are just newer than others."

Cody studied his face for a moment. "Jim Jones said, 'If you see me as your God, then I'll be your God.' That line of his has always stuck with me. What if someone had a new Jonestown situation goin' on down here? Would you necessarily know about it? Someone told me you get around this state quite a bit." Cody could imagine the Andersons were now thinking hard about Jonestown, even though he hadn't met them. Any parent whose child disappeared in Central America or Chiapas couldn't help thinking about that.

Artemio Díaz set his glass down on the table between them. "Just because we're in the jungle or the pine forest doesn't mean we're vulnerable to that sort of thing now. That would be the exception, not the rule. Anyway, think of all the cults that didn't end like that. Jonestown was unique, fortunately."

"That was down in Guyana, I believe. That's not so far from here."

"Far enough. A couple thousand miles, anyway. But those people that died there were almost entirely Americans, weren't they? That's a long time ago now."

"In the late seventies. I was a very young cop then."

"Most people aren't so crazy these days, even the Americans. Well, I guess they still are, but not so much about religion. It's more about politics now. Religion is not my field, anyway. I'm only a mechanic. The human body is my machine of choice."

Both were silent for a while. Cody had seen plenty of craziness in his role with the Agency. They were sitting in the overgrown courtyard of Artemio Díaz' house behind the cathedral. It had once been a fine proud place to live, even elegant, with tall ceilings and detailed cornices, a handful of keystone arches at the courtyard entrances on all four sides. They reflected a North African influence that had traveled this far via Spain. Now no one interfered with what the garden wished to be, an objective that varied with every plant, vine, and tree. The only shared goal was to reach above the surrounding four walls and bask in the sun's intermittent appearances. Below, the courtyard offered no shortage of shade even in mid afternoon.

"I suspect you are looking for someone in particular, my friend, not just a cult of the usual dreamers," said Díaz, not looking at Cody. "But you are thinking that I wouldn't want to help you if you had told me that straight out. You must try to trust me a bit more."

Cody nodded, as there was no denying this. "My reluctance in saying so was that for people to trust you out in the bush you would need a strong sense of discretion. You can't be carrying tales from one village to another. I wanted to ease into it. I'm discreet too."

"You are correct in trying to think like a Mexican.

My role is always to be neither troubadour nor telegraph wire. Trust is important on both sides. The Maya do not see me as one of their traditional healers, a *curandero* or a shaman, so that is a hurdle too. Who is this person you wish to find?"

Cody reached into his shirt pocket and pulled out an unaltered copy of the information sheet the Agency had gotten from Garrett Anderson. Across the top were the three photos of Megan.

Díaz studied it for a moment before he slowly began to nod without expression. "Yes, I have seen this woman, and I believe I know where she is, at least where she was last month, although she does not use this name anymore. I hadn't heard it before."

Cody frowned. This was not going to make things any easier. "What name is she using now?"

"Jalanme'tik ta Banomil."

"What?" Cody looked at him sharply. "That must be a local name. How odd that she would choose that."

"It's not so odd for the place she is in now. It's from the Tzotzil language, one of more than thirty Mayan tongues."

"What does it mean? Or is it just something new?" Cody could see how Megan might be cultivating a fresh identity if she had discovered an inspiring situation.

"You might want to ask her that yourself, my

friend. Some people like to cast away the past and re-invent themselves, you know? That is what this young woman has done. But aren't you doing that too? You told me you are living in San Miguel. Many Americans living in México wish to accomplish that. We should not be surprised to see her doing this. All of us have our own path, even in the high pine forest."

Cody did not respond immediately. "Is she in good health?"

Díaz shrugged. "I have not examined her, and she has spoken to me of no health complaints. Of course, she is young. I should tell you I have met her only once."

Cody nodded slowly, pondering the leap from Swedish or Norwegian to Tzotzil without success. "Where is she?"

"She is living in a large but obscure village called Mazintla, far away in the highlands beyond Ocosingo. You will never find it, and even if you knew where it was you would probably not be able to reach it."

"So she has gone to Shangri-la?"

Díaz shook his head soberly. "Well, it is not Shangri-la, not by a long shot. What kind of vehicle do you use?"

"Three of us are traveling in a two-year-old Chrysler Town & Country."

Artemio Díaz shook his head more vigorously, even as he chuckled. "You will never get through with that. The road is what they call difficult, even for Chiapas. To start, you would need much higher ground clearance. There is no paving and it is full of rocks and gullies. You might have to get out and push in some places, and the washouts can be very dangerous. The valleys are far below."

This seemed to give Cody an idea. "What do you drive when you go there? I assume you have a patient or two you visit."

"More than a few in that area, and I remain for several days at a time when I go. I use a Land Rover. It's an older one, but it gets me through. This young woman is a relative of yours?"

"No. We're working for her parents." Cody hated to admit it, but it appeared that the Zacher Agency was going to have to be more forthcoming to get the kind of help they needed. After their experience trekking through the Yucatán jungle, hacking out each foot of progress in search of a ruined Mayan temple, none of them wanted to tackle the wilderness again without the aid of a guide and better equipment.

"You will need some assistance in getting there. Also, the local people would require an introduction. They don't look kindly on strangers who walk in out of the bush, as if any could. None of you could speak their language. The village headman would have to approve you." Díaz looked at him steadily. "You must realize that the Maya have never fully submitted to outsiders, whether the Spanish in the sixteenth century or anyone else in all the years that followed. Mazintla is deep inside the autonomous zones. You will find no official presence there that is not strictly local. They do not recognize either the state or the federal government."

"Then I can also imagine they don't see many visitors."

"Which is as they wish." Díaz shrugged and finished his drink. "Of course I am always welcome there."

"So you must speak Tzotzil."

Díaz responded with an incomprehensible paragraph followed by a laugh.

"I'll take that as yes. What would it cost for you to take three of us there? I'm sure you could use a contribution for medications and supplies." Certainly the indigenous people couldn't afford to pay Artemio Díaz much, or at all.

"I am thinking I would take you there for $1,000 U.S."

Cody was surprised. "But this is México. That's not a Mexican price."

"Right, but most of the supplies still have to come down here from the States, a place where all the health care providers are rich. Who will take care of these people if I do not? I am not a wealthy man anymore, Señor Williams. I have long ago spent my pot of gold on my patients."

The budget for their $8,000 deposit from the Andersons had not included anything like that for a guide. Cody had been thinking to offer a fifth of what Díaz was asking.

"Let me consult the others on this and I'll get back to you shortly."

CHAPTER FIVE

O n Cody's return, the email I sent to Garrett Anderson was concise, and a copy went to his attorney, who did not acknowledge it, at least to us.

"We have found a local doctor who believes he knows where Megan is. She's living in a remote Mayan village in the highlands of the interior, one that our vehicle cannot reach because the road is so poorly maintained. Besides this obstacle, we will need a guide to locate it and to translate for us once we arrive, since the locals speak only Tzotzil, one of the ancient Mayan languages. Will you provide a donation of $1,000 U.S. to his medical charity work in exchange for the doctor providing these services?"

The response was rapid and equally straightforward.

"You're telling me that this guy is a doctor? That quack must have seen you coming. Besides demanding an outrageous price, how do you know he won't take the money (my money!) and dump you off somewhere in the jungle where you'll never be heard from again?"

I admit I had exaggerated the problem in my email, but not by much. Dr. Díaz had told Cody that it was mainly the older generation that spoke only Tzotzil, and people middle-aged and younger also spoke Spanish. But the underlying idea was correct—we weren't likely to get to Megan without expert help, and the pool of potential guides to draw from was not large. How she'd found her way to a remote place like Mazintla herself was something we could ask her when we located her.

We took a vote. Enjoying Garrett Anderson's word as an addition to her English slang vocabulary, Maya suggested we ought to *dump* the Andersons as lacking sufficient flexibility to pull off this kind of project. Cody, having done the Díaz interview, pled for patience and suggested that I furnish a more careful (meaning diplomatic) explanation to our client.

I was neutral, thinking that the Andersons could probably be brought around with some further effort, but on the other hand, why should we have to coddle them on every unanticipated factor that popped up as the case developed? Had we been hired so they could second-guess everything we did? There are people out there, and we'd met a few of them on other cases, who simply have to be superior to everything and everyone they encounter, especially when the outcome is less than perfect. We had never achieved perfection yet. Furthermore, I was certain that there would be no shortage of other nasty and unexpected challenges coming our way, as they always did, so why allow the Andersons to add to that pile on whatever whim they might come up with?

In the end, I suppose my position won. Whether that would turn out to be a victory worth celebrating was an open question. I was charged with bringing the Andersons around through diplomacy while letting them know at the same time that we didn't care to operate on such a short leash. Also, the three of us were old México hands and not about to be easily taken in by some upcountry quack. México has plenty of cynical people waiting to skim a few bucks off the gringos, and it doesn't take long to be able to spot them. Some greater degree of trust of the Agency by its clients was required. I planned to add in my response that we wouldn't have referred the thousand-dollar fee issue to them unless we also supported it to begin with. What I wasn't planning to say yet was that without Díaz' help I thought we were already finished with the Megan Anderson disappearance case.

And this was the substance of what I told her parents in my reply. I didn't include the fact that I believed they could afford to give a little extra to Díaz because his cause was so worthwhile; that was an extraneous matter. Besides, I couldn't think of another way to get into Mazintla and find Megan, if that's where she still was. Without the aid of Díaz, pricy or not, we would be staying on for a while in San Cristobal as tourists, and then we'd be back on the road home.

It wasn't that we couldn't have found another guide to take us there; I also wanted one who had *seen* Megan there. I didn't believe that blindly battling our way through the high-altitude pine forest to some off-trail backwater with primitive guest facilities, if any, and hanging around looking for a woman none of us had ever seen before was the best way to do this. Not that we couldn't pick her out of a crowd of the highland Maya, but if there was an active cult going on there, might it not be cloaked in secrecy? And who was to say that if it had lured Megan in, why wouldn't there be other young blond women present? It was possible that Megan wouldn't be acknowledging her old name at all anymore. A town that looked like a dead end to us could perfectly well appear to be a desirable destination to an inexperienced young Minnesotan who didn't know this country and might think it was quaint or exotic.

Four or five hours of online silence followed my carefully drafted answer, as if a debate was raging on the other end. Finally this came in: *"All right, then go ahead. G. A."* I could read his scowl between the lines.

"Zina pulled him up short," Maya suggested. "She was looking over his shoulder as he wrote that. Your original email caught him in a nasty mood about something else and he took it out on you as the nearest target."

"It must have been about money," Cody added. "Sometimes it's no more than the timing of a message that makes you run into someone else's quarrel."

But the timing was right even so, because the thousand-dollar transfer hit the Agency account at the end of business that day.

CHAPTER SIX

We were about as eager to depart San Cristobal for the jungle as to have a root canal, but Artemio Díaz was leaving on his monthly village rounds in two days.

"This is reminding me of our trip north of Valladolid in the Yucatán," said Maya. "The coral snakes were dropping out of the trees onto our necks."

"Except for the one I sliced in half with my machete on the way down," Cody said.

"Don't remind me."

"Only the back half of it hit you."

We had packed all our immediate needs into Cody's suitcase, and stored the other one at our hotel, since the back of Díaz' Land Rover would be filled with supplies for his medical mission and his own gear. He intended to be gone about ten days, which would cover three stops. The first would be Mazintla. We planned to follow him almost as far as a small, unpaved highway exit about sixteen kilometers above Ocosingo. It was located two kilometers past a cantina called El Toro Verde, the Green Bull, where Díaz said he sometimes stopped for a dose of courage before embarking on the harrowing last leg of the trip into Mazintla, which he described as about seventy kilometers of near-death experience. Díaz knew the cantina manager from his frequent stops there. It was the last place to get a decent meal before Mazintla, and he said we'd be able to leave the hopeless van with the manager and continue with him in the Land Rover. When Díaz left Mazintla for the next leg of his medical circuit three days later, we could ride back to the highway with him and pick up the van while he continued north.

It was a simple plan. Whether or not we'd have Megan Anderson with us, we couldn't see far enough ahead to assess. At a minimum we'd be able to tell the Andersons where she was and what she was doing. Maybe for a small upcharge Díaz could add a report on her health. Hopefully we could also bring back her message to them if she hadn't returned with us and there was a problem with communications infrastructure that far out in the bush. If she did elect to stay, the Anderson's could share in the responsibility, since that would mean she hadn't responded to the note they'd given us to deliver to her.

There was also no question of putting her on a plane anywhere within fifteen hours of Mazintla. The only "nearby" airports were at Tuxtla Gutierrez in

Chiapas, an hour and a half beyond San Cristobal by car, or at Villahermosa in the state of Tabasco, all the way across Chiapas to the east. This all sounded too sketchy to us, but we had no alternatives. We had tried both Megan's email and her cell several times from San Cristobal but we could never get any response.

Although it had seemed prudently elastic at the time we took the case, it was now, in the field, making all of us a little queasy that we'd never defined precisely what would constitute success. I thought that simply finding Megan might have to be enough if she wouldn't return with us. I could think of no reason that she would. Just getting to Mazintla was an achievement she might well be proud of. In that case we'd take a few cell phone photos of her posed with one of us to prove we'd located her alive and well.

Since we had crossed into Chiapas from Oaxaca, we'd encountered jungle at the lower levels, then cloud forest at four to six thousand feet, which was a mixture of pine and deciduous trees, especially oak. Now, within a few kilometers of leaving San Cristobal's valley setting, the topography became mountainous and twisted, all densely wooded with tall long-needle pine. The astringent scent of it hung in misty ragged sheets and slowed us to a crawling pace around one hairpin curve after another. The filmy quality of the light read more like dusk than morning. Often on one side of the road the terrain was straight up and the other side straight down. At the edges of the deep valleys we occasionally glimpsed large blocks of palm oil plantings marching up the slopes. In other places we spotted a few rows of corn, trekking up the burned-off hillsides and funneling the topsoil down into the bottomland below. We never knew what awaited us around a corner. At one turn, heralded by a column of dense black smoke, we came across a car burning furiously on the edge of the road. Eager flames filled the entire vehicle, front to back. No one was visible inside. Had someone settled an argument this way? Were there people still inside the car, their remains now incinerated on the floor?

As if this were the normal course of events in Chiapas, Díaz had not paused to investigate. Maya was squirming uneasily in back, but she didn't voice any concern other than a tight-lipped mutter that sounded like, "Don't slow down, don't slow down." Cody and I kept our own counsel, not wanting to speculate on the meaning of what we'd seen.

We passed several small clusters of buildings too fragmentary to call hamlets, barely clinging to level spaces along the slopes. Determined turkeys poked in the weeds along the edges of the road. Coffee bushes, with their tiny white flowers, grew everywhere. Some buildings displayed huge political slogans supporting the ELZN painted on the façades of shops and even houses, the acronym for the Zapatista Army of National Liberation. We encountered no regular military vehicles, like those we often saw on the road in other places throughout México. Crossing no visible boundaries, we had entered one of the autonomous zones. It was not obvious what, if anything, had changed. The few people we encountered looked no different. We saw no black-masked Zapatistas. No one was carrying semi-automatic weapons. The clouds of mist swirled, merged, separated, and merged again, but never opened out into blue, which would've offered a kind of relief from a landscape that was starting to feel more and more isolated and oppressive.

"Strange terrain," said Cody after a long silence. "This is not the México I know, and I've been all around this country. These people are living in the clouds."

"But it's not uplifting," said Maya.

"I wonder if this is a way of getting closer to heaven for Megan." I was thinking aloud. "Even if it's not very inviting, I can see how it might feel spiritual to someone who's searching. It's not quite real, in spite of the obvious poverty."

Yet there were widely separated interruptions in the filmy fabric of this fantasy. It felt transitory and only half formed. We happily arrived in Ocosingo to find an interesting valley town with a substantial cluster of Mayan ruins on one side that we didn't have time to visit. Possibly on our return, since it could be a pleasant break. Several large arcaded buildings fronted the plaza. I couldn't tell whether we were back in normally governed México or not. Ahead of us, Díaz slowed down only enough to refuel once. In this part of the country a gas station was usually a house with several rows of translucent white plastic gas containers waiting out front. The gasoline itself showed like a pink shadow within.

When we reached El Toro Verde cantina north of town it wasn't doing much business for an early afternoon. In the States we would've called it a roadhouse. There were no other buildings around it. Streamers of mist drifted past in the bottomless valley behind it. I was nervous about leaving the van with the bar owner, but aside from two Shakira CDs and a few others, and a sheaf of maps, it was empty of our gear once we transferred Cody's well-used leather suitcase into the Land Rover. I parked the Town & Country on a narrow strip behind the cantina, as far in from the edge as I could, dropped off the keys with the manager so he could move it if he had to, and settled into Artemio Díaz' Land Rover, thinking that some family with three kids would probably be living in the van when we returned. Nothing goes to waste here.

The turnoff to Mazintla and other isolated points in the veiled no man's land ahead looked like it had never been more than a rock-strewn track through the clouds, full of small muddy gullies to lurch over. A better transport vehicle would have been a helicopter mounted with a strong searchlight. After about twelve slow kilometers we reached a fork where the left branch went to Toniná. There was no sign informing us of that, but Díaz told us this as if it meant something important. I decided he was only trying to comfort us with the idea that Mazintla was not the last outpost of civilization. Clearly, the traveler who did not have a precise destination in mind had no business at all on this single lane path.

Mercifully, a thin row of weepy, long-needle pines largely screened both margins of the ridge from view. This was reassuring, even though we knew we were tracing the course of a knife-edge spine that wandered among precipitous drop-offs. What kind of penitent pilgrimage was Megan Anderson embarked on, that would entice her into this National Geographic nightmare? It was the kind of setting where their camera crews could disappear in a blink. Whatever Garrett Anderson's impression of his daughter's state of mind had been, Megan could never have been some tentative fair flower if she successfully tackled this route. You had to admire her nerve for taking on what felt like a thinly forested moonscape.

The well-worn interior of the ten-year-old Land Rover had been clean when he started, said Díaz, slightly apologetic. Now it was coated with road dust and grit. The interior plastic surfaces were all cracked and splitting. The black leather seats under us were alligatored and ripped at the corners. Maya sat in back with me, her hands in her pockets as if trying to avoid touching anything. On the frequent corkscrew curves we lurched against each other.

"Not much like San Miguel, is it?" said Díaz, cheerfully, as if near death experiences were the new normal. "I was up there once three years ago to make a speech to get donations. I showed them a little movie, too."

"How did you do?" said Cody.

"I came back with a bit more than two thousand dollars. It was worth it. Too many gringos though, up there. I thought I was in Texas. This is the real México." His left arm reached out of the window to embrace its moist and nebulous charm.

"If this was the real México," I said, "I would've stayed in Ohio. It's beautiful, but how do people manage to live here?"

"The same way they always did. Most of the houses have little garden plots, and they keep chickens and turkeys and other animals. You will see this when we arrive to Mazintla." Díaz switched the windshield wipers on and off quickly to clear the glass of the condensed vapor that had begun to stream off to the sides.

"When was your last trip here?" asked Maya.

"Last month. I go every month like this."

"Is there a hotel?" I said.

Both hands flew up in a gesture suggesting how approximate that term was. I nearly reached past him to steady the wheel. "Ah, not exactly. There is a room with hammocks, you will see, where you can all stay together, family style. The main corridor has a bathroom. I stay with the village headman because I am an honored guest. They have no other medical care. I fix their dogs too, when I have time."

"And this is more rewarding than your other career," Cody said.

"Absolutely, and it's all done for free. No one pays me a peso."

"What about the religious group?" said Maya.

"Well, that's interesting. They have had a fight and they split up into two groups now. One part took over the old church and the other built a new place down the slope. It's kind of a shack. So they don't talk to each other any more, and some families are divided. It's not so good for the village. But that's often the way of religion, you know? That's why I prefer science. The truth of it changes all the time, but no one fights over it."

"Which part did Megan Anderson choose?"

"You mean Jalanme'tik ta Banomil? She is part of the group that stayed with the old church building. They have a service every evening, so you will probably be able to find her tonight."

A battered red fifteen-year-old Chevrolet pickup with knobby oversize tires approached from the other direction and we veered to one side, hugging the trees. The branches scraped Cody's door. Díaz could have shaken hands with the other driver without leaning out his window. Through the barrier of sentinel pines I could make out the patchwork of tiny fields in the valley far below. Their colors were muted, as if filtered by distance. From that height it looked like a map without much detail. I had no way of knowing, but the drop from there could easily have been more than a thousand meters.

"Does anyone want to pause and look at the view?" Díaz asked with a grin. He had too much gusto in treating us as greenhorns, I thought.

"Just go, please," said Maya, "go, go. We've seen too much of this view already. I will never forget it."

After another two and a half hours the track gradually sloped downward and we came to a stop near the bottom of the dip. There the road had crumbled away on the right side into a V shaped gulley that started at a point in the middle of the track. It widened as it spilled off over the slope through a gap in the row of trees that once must have been filled. What remained of the road was too narrow to support both sides of the Land Rover. Maya covered her eyes, murmuring something I couldn't make out. Although she never prayed, she was a long-time master of incoherent muttering.

"Not to worry," said Díaz, over his shoulder. "It's always like this, or something like it." To me, his cheerful voice had a hollow sound. We all got out, hugging the single row of pines on the driver's side. It felt safer outside of the Land Rover. About fifteen or twenty planks and saplings stripped of branches lay scattered at the edge of the road, and someone had stacked more along the trees. It was reassuring to think that the pickup we had just passed had to have come this way, so it must be possible, even if chancy and foolhardy. We helped Díaz rearrange the planks in two layers in a kind of diagonal crosshatching over the pointed part of the gap. He seemed to know what he was doing. The planks were cold and wet to the touch. To be that slippery on our hands meant they would also be quite slippery to the tires. I couldn't help but see us slide right over the side where I tried not to look as streamers of chilly wet haze rolled over us. We wiped our hands off on our pants and climbed back in.

"Are you a man of faith?" said Cody, shivering, again seated next to Díaz. The world around us seemed strangely silent, as if anticipating our screams.

"Sure. I have total faith in seasoned English all terrain vehicles. How about you?"

"I'm learning how to pray again right now."

"Then it's too bad you don't know Tzotzil, since that's the language of the gods up here. Without it you don't have much of a chance of making contact. If you call out for Christ no one answers."

I pressed Maya's hand in mine. She gave me a twisted look. My abdomen was as rigid as if it were tightly packed with stone. It suddenly occurred to me that all three of us could've crossed the break in the road on foot and joined Díaz on the other side, but it seemed rude and lacking in confidence to suggest that. I comforted myself by thinking that if he thought the risk too serious he would've brought that up himself.

We backed up about ten meters and Díaz stomped on the gas pedal with a ritual shout, as if he was part Cherokee and it came back to him in stressful moments like this. I stopped breathing. When the front tires hit the near edge of the planks the other ends lifted for one sickening instant as if about to flee in alarm. Then they slammed down hard as we rattled and bounced over the makeshift roadbed, clearing the gap. I saw only one sapling go over the side, spinning end over end.

"Jesus Christ," said Cody, rubbing his face vigorously. "I only want to do that one more time before I die."

"I wish Garry and Zina could've seen that," Maya said. "They probably think they're paying us too much."

As if that adventure had earned us the right of admission into Mazintla, only one further kilometer up the slope we entered the edge of town. The narrow road widened onto a nearly level plateau. The trees mostly retreated to the edges, and a gaggle of pigs and turkeys came out to meet us, all expressing a raucous greeting that was neither Spanish nor Tzotzil, but something more universal.

"What did you bring us?" they were saying. Any arrival was a fiesta. Díaz pulled a handful of dry corn kernels out of a bag in the door pocket next to his seat and tossed it into the crowd with a practiced flick of his wrist. This drew them out of our path and we triumphantly cruised into Mazintla. Three of us, at least, could've wept with relief.

CHAPTER SEVEN
IN THE DEN OF THE *BRUJA*

I'd already seen too many of the poorer parts of México, but this town took poverty a few degrees farther than most. We didn't see many cars, but the ones we came across were mostly dead, up on blocks, or settled in place on defeated tires. No building we passed had been painted recently, and the unpaved streets were hollowed with muddy potholes. I tried to imagine why this was the pilgrimage destination for Megan Anderson, the upscale Edina coed, and Leo Cochrane, the missionary boy dressed in a tie, khaki slacks, and a button down shirt, that her parents had mentioned as her companion going south. Yet hope is the feedstock of religion, and hope may have been the only commodity of value that remained to the local people in any quantity.

In spite of this, or perhaps because of it, each cultural subgroup develops its own look, especially among the Maya, who have always been determinedly local in their outlook and appearance. The next thing I noticed in this isolated village was the women's hairstyles. At the widest portion it was flat on top, with a part than ran straight front to back. The hair itself was tightly curled in a dense mass tapering downward like wings toward the neck. Only the younger girls and the older women had a more natural cut.

"What is this look?" said Maya, leaning forward.

"It's just the style of this place," said Díaz over his shoulder. "They get that kinky effect from the bark on some shrub; I don't know which one. I guess they have to do it as a rinse a couple of times each week. Otherwise it straightens out by its own. The girls adopt this look at puberty and wear it until they're widowed."

"And are they usually widowed?" said Maya softly, as if the answer held the key to some lethal element running loose here.

"Sure. The men drink a lot. Sometimes they fight. There's nothing else to do. They make their own *pulque*, and to bring in the cheap vodka and tequila by motorcycle is an important job."

Other than this hairstyle there seemed to be no special group costume except that the women also wore two squares or ovals of finely woven palm fronds on their chest over a variety of normal shirts or blouses. The range of shapes and decorative bindings on the edges of these breastplates suggested a creative outlet that didn't cost much to practice. In San Cristobal we had also seen a number of distinctive local dress styles among women from outlying villages that came into town to sell crafts. The men we saw in Mazintla were dressed in no consistent manner.

I didn't notice any central market, but we passed a number of small fruit and vegetable stands selling what must have been homegrown produce. Certainly in this misty, cool climate leaf crops would do well.

About five blocks in we passed a small plaza. Aside from a ring of pines in the center that shaded half a dozen benches, and a single broad, weeping long-needle pine tree on each corner, we saw no other landscaping. I wondered who needed any shade, since the sky appeared to offer little else. A pack of about a dozen dogs was lounging about with nothing much going on. The temperature was just comfortable, no warmer. The open areas in the plaza were sparsely covered with weedy soil that appeared to be raked in the bare places that had little traffic.

Facing one side was a typical stucco church that may have been large enough to accommodate four hundred people. The front doors were closed and there was no activity around it. Was this where we would later connect with Megan Anderson?

"What's the population here?" said Cody.

"About three thousand."

Three thousand people, I thought, with no

doctor except for Díaz' monthly circuit. Nor was there a nearby hospital or clinic or any dental care, obviously. The word *nearby* had no real meaning here. You could describe the distance from Mazintla back to the highway in kilometers, but that did no justice at all to the process of getting there.

On the corner nearest the church an old woman sat in the shade on a green plastic chair with a soft drink logo on the back. Her straight white hair was trimmed short. On a tripod grill full of burning coals she was preparing *gorditas*, placing each finished one on a platter covered by a coarsely fringed cloth. No one came near her as we crawled past. At the base of one of the trees nearer the center a table was set up display-ing used clothing for sale, some of it pinned to the shaggy bark in lifelike positions. This was merchandising, I thought.

Half a block off the plaza, which was surrounded by the only cobblestone street we had seen, we pulled up at a single story house with peeling stucco and a rusty wrought iron grid securing the door. The building appeared to have once been more upscale than its neighbors, or it may only have been a bit larger. The front door was painted a watery blue full of puckered linear cracks that exposed the pale bare wood beneath. Patches of sun suddenly appeared. When Díaz got out and rang the bell the dark wooden shutters on the single barred window opened. A nearly toothless man looked through it and then shuffled out to let us in a long moment later.

When the door swung open I introduced us and gave him my card. He eagerly welcomed us. As we stepped inside, I had to wonder how much business he ever got. Several tall windows opened out to the inner courtyard from the white-painted corridor we walked through. This outdoor space was bare of any organized planting. It looked like whatever seeds blew over the wall were welcomed and allowed to take root.

"I hope this works for you," said Díaz. "The new twenty-story Hilton has not started construction here yet. You can reach me at the headman's house. Anyone will take a message there for a peso. The children with shoes are the message runners." Maya stood with her hands on her hips as if lost.

By the time we said goodbye to Díaz as Cody brought in our suitcase, dusk was approaching. Our host led us further down the corridor and we stopped at the second of three doors. Inside a medium-sized room four hammocks waited anchored between the walls and four stone columns that stood further into the room. A cream-colored wool blanket was folded up on each one, but no pillow was offered. Four white plastic chairs lined the outer wall, which had three horizontal windows near the ceiling on the courtyard side. In one corner sat a matching plastic table set with two oil lamps and an ash-tray that needed emptying. The cost was ninety pesos for the three of us, a little more than five dollars per night. This was not going to present any problem for Garrett Anderson's budget. The old man gave us a key to the entry, but none for the room, and left us alone with a cheerful wave.

We stowed our single suitcase in one corner and stared at each other.

"I guess this is all right," Cody said, with the hint of a frown.

"I'm surprised there's anything at all," Maya said. "Driving in I thought we'd be staying at someone's house and it wouldn't be even this good."

After what we'd gone through to get there I felt like the outcome was completely anticlimactic. If we couldn't locate Megan in Mazintla, we'd have nothing at all to offer Garrett Anderson other than an expense list. No one wanted to linger in the room, so we used the bathroom, which was marginal, if clean, and launched an exploratory ramble carrying a few apples and other snacks we had brought. None of us felt like searching for a restaurant—the idea that there might even be one seemed naïve. After circling three or four blocks to get our bearings—they looked hardly any different and none of the streets had names—we walked back to the plaza and crossed to the church entry, where a few people were now standing around chatting as others went in.

Looking like wrestlers, three short heavily built guards screened the entering traffic at the doors. They must have been selected from the congregation, and their weight didn't look much like muscle, it was more like tortillas. It was clear from the sour expression on their faces that as strangers we didn't make the cut for admission. I wondered why they needed that much security. How many visitors ever got as far as Mazintla? If travelers weren't spooked enough by the deteriorated condition of the road itself, the breach that nearly cut it in two below the town would act like a moat for most prudent explorers.

"It could be that some bad feelings still persist from the split," Cody suggested, folding his arms. We were all now standing in the street about five meters from the church doors. At that distance the security men ignored us. The shadows were lengthening rapidly, since the sun had recently tumbled into the valley below. "I also want to check out that other half of the cult before we leave this town."

From inside the church the beat of drums and chanting came up, with a brace of flutes weaving through the rhythms. The scent of incense wafted toward us, since the outer doors were open, but within, a second set of doors with frosted glass in the upper half, open to the vaulted ceiling above, kept us from seeing the action. The appearance of the well-used church was unadorned eighteenth century, with weathered door casings of smooth, unembellished *cantera* limestone. Near the peak of the façade a small niche housed a bell, and below it read 1787 in dark blue letters on a white oval ceramic tablet.

While the proportions of this old church were graceful, the surfaces were utilitarian. Two hundred years later we would've seen the identical no-frills message in unpainted cinder block without the same grace of proportion. We took a seat on a park bench facing the entry and waited for a blond Minnesota woman to walk in.

After half an hour without seeing her, Maya and I left Cody in position to keep up the watch while we went searching for another exit. I glanced around the plaza behind us, but no lights had come on yet on any side of it. It felt like dusk arrived early and heavily here, as if there was no nightlife at all beyond church meetings.

"What do people do here for amusement?" Maya said, taking my hand.

"They pray." I said softly. "They pray for something to happen, anything."

"And what can Megan Anderson possibly find to interest her in this? Where she came from in Edina the world was an upscale consumer place. What I remember most is that it's all about shopping and car dealers and high-end restaurants. I can still see it." The trip to Minnesota on our initial case had been Maya's first visit to the United States.

"Right. From what we saw then it's about who has the biggest riding lawn mower. Who can spend the most money embellishing his house with phony gables. I don't know what Megan could find to reward her presence here. She could probably buy a house on a big lot in this town for cash with one month of her trust fund income. I don't feel anything mystical or spiritual at all about this place." I could only shake my head. Maybe Megan found something uplifting in poverty, the pure of heart kind of thing, blessed be the humble and all that, but I couldn't see the connection because I'd already seen far too much of it in México. Maya and I had few extravagances, other than her horse, and we had plenty to eat and wear, but I saw nothing to admire about the Mazintla lifestyle. Being beaten down like this could only be depressing.

Maya and I walked around to the left side of the church where near the far end was a smaller single door that opened onto an arcaded stone-paved walkway leading to a parish house ten meters away. The unpretentious residence was also done in pale green stucco like the church, but it was in a better state of repair. It was also one of the few two-story buildings we had seen in town. On the ground in the center of each of six arches along both sides of this passage an oil lamp burned. In the space between the buildings the twilight was thickening around us. From the corner of my eye I saw a bat dart into the space between two tiles in the arcade roof. Maya shivered and rubbed her arms.

"Not what you thought, is it?" I said, putting one arm around her shoulders.

"It never is. I should've realized that."

With the failure of the light a mild breeze came up. As odd as it was to feel chilly this far south, I was glad I'd brought a denim jacket. Part of it was the altitude; we were higher than eight thousand feet. Maya was wearing her short white quilted coat, no longer perfectly clean, and as we waited she pulled her collar up and shoved her hands in her pockets. After another ten minutes the service fell silent and the side door swung open. A different burly security guard came out, paused, looked over the area, and not discovering much to worry about from Maya and me, continued toward the parish house door, where he pulled out a set of keys and opened it. Then he turned back to watch the small church door, his arms behind him.

After a moment a light-skinned woman emerged onto the arcaded walkway. Her blond hair was massed in the same tightly curled shape we had seen throughout the village; flat on top on both sides of a straight part and tapering down to just below her ears. Within the blackened hollows of her eye sockets her blue eyes gleamed. She was wearing a long, gauzy, translucent white wraparound skirt that lifted on the air, and the oil lamps on the pavers lit the contour of her legs and lower torso within. From the waist up she was naked but for a pair of square woven palm frond plaques edged in gold thread and joined in the center by a fiber link. They hung from a chain at her neck and were secured at the bottom corners by a cord that was tied behind her bare back. She did not appear to be shivering.

Beneath these woven squares her full round breasts swelled outward along all four edges. Maya froze in mid step, gasped, and whispered in my ear, "Megan Anderson! But what is she wearing?"

From behind her a much shorter local woman emerged from the church door bearing a long robe with both hands. She draped it over Megan's shoulders. Mauve in color, it appeared to be satin and was entirely embroidered with floral motifs in a wide range of colors.

I immediately stepped closer as Megan paused to fasten it at her throat. She did not look at me until I spoke to her.

"Are you the local *bruja*?" I said in English. I didn't want to call her Megan, but at that moment I couldn't remember her new name in Tzotzil, and even if I had I couldn't have pronounced it.

She paused, unsurprised. "If that's what you

need me to be, then I am." Her voice was a hoarse whisper, as if she had just come from making herself heard over a large and noisy gathering.

Her gaze met mine without faltering. Aside from the startling masklike eye treatment, she wore little makeup. I didn't need to remove the data and photo sheet from my shirt pocket to be sure it truly was Megan Anderson. Despite the radical change in presentation I could still see the heritage of Minnesota glowing in the purely Scandinavian skin tones of her arms and bare shoulders, in her minimally tinted lips, and in her pale eyebrows. Perhaps that was her exotic appeal in this dreary, isolated place, where, aside from liberal doses of alcohol, religion was the only source of spirit or of hope. My first impression of her was that she owned no part of this dull and stunting reality, but floated above it like an angel or a saint. The local hair treatment done as a blond said she was part of this inaccessible village, but of a different social rank; perhaps the mother goddess of them all. I thought of Cortés' arrival in Tenochtitlan in 1519. The Aztecs thought him a god too.

Maya remained silent, as if waiting for more from both of us.

From her father's sketchy description I recalled that Megan was twenty-four years old. I was at once attracted and repelled by her appearance. Hers was a strong face that would wear well as she got older.

Although you could call it beautiful in its features, it was neither soft nor yielding in the indifferent glow of the oil lamps. She appeared to carry the authority of her role without stress or any great effort. Still, beneath her artificial appearance the impression began to slowly grow on me that she had tapped into a deep and arcane tradition to which I could not have given any name. I read this from a kind of eloquent serenity in her eyes. Standing as near to her as I was, I felt a kind of energy come off her. Even wearing this bizarre costume, and in this crumbling shantytown on the edge of the world, she was at home within herself.

I took a single step backward. There was clearly far more going on with Megan than what her father had suggested to us. It may have been the strain of mysticism that he had missed. Perhaps he had no such quality in himself and therefore couldn't recognize it in others.

From her profile as she stood there, awaiting my response with her lips slightly parted, I also realized she was about six months pregnant.

CHAPTER EIGHT

"My father is a tyrannical asshole," Jalanme'tik ta Banomil said calmly as we sat in her parochial parlor. This was not her opening line but it was the one that captured the attention of all of us. From her tone, this was far from the first time she'd said it. She had begun by telling us her new name meant Mother Goddess of the Earth, but we didn't have to use it on merely social occasions like this, only if we entered the church when she was present. After that it took a while for her to open up, and I sensed that the question in her mind was whether we were allies of her father, or there as people who were still capable of making their own judgment on what we were looking at. It was also possible that it simply took her a while to wind down after a meeting like the one she'd just conducted.

"Nice promotion," Cody said, gesturing to the surroundings, "and only six months after getting your bachelor's degree."

"Thanks, I know." She shrugged as if that were

a different story. "Maybe you already realized how my father acts just from talking to him. My mother has never had the backbone to resist him. It's always, 'Yes, Garry,' or, 'Of course, Garry. Do you think you'd like dinner now, Garry?'"

Maya had collected Cody from the front of the church as soon as Megan invited us in after hearing of our mission. After disappearing for a moment to change, she was now wearing a wrinkled loose-fitting blue cotton skirt that came to just below her knees, scuffed and soiled tan suede athletic shoes without socks, and an oversize green and white Edina athletic department sweatshirt that bulged over her abdomen. The message was *GO HORNETS*. Her makeup was unchanged. The look was one I'd call informal cult goddess after hours. I was relieved that despite her hair and eyes she had mostly unwound into the Minnesota girl she originally was. Maya looked relieved too. She could never have dealt with a full time deity that didn't ever switch it off.

"Did *you* resist him?" Cody asked. "Your father?"

"Subtly. It doesn't pay to go head to head with him. The problem was he could never see what I am; he could only see what he wanted me to be. The biggest part of that was that he had wanted me to be a boy. I know that's a cliché, but it's only a cliché because it happens so often. My mother was not able to have any more kids after I was born, so he had to settle for what I was, not that he ever did. They didn't consider adopting because they thought it was a crapshoot with bad odds. Still, nothing I ever did growing up was quite right, either, and I'm sure he sees my going to México in that same light."

The once-formal parsonage parlor was furnished with an ancient well-worn sofa bearing torn plum-colored velvet upholstery, parts of it on the seat polished to a threadbare sheen from hard use. A dozen and a half straight-back pine chairs with wicker seats were stationed along the bruised and faded stenciled walls, as if the room had often been used for overcrowded church business meetings. Above the chairs the walls displayed an incompatible variety of pious but dog-eared Catholic prints, local floral embroideries, and a couple of primitive woodcarvings of unusual saints in the ever-present unstained pine.

Through the grilled windows facing the plaza the darkness had deepened outside, but only five small oil lamps lit our surroundings. It reminded me of the ethereal gaslight interiors the Victorians were accustomed to. Shadows collected thickly in all the corners of the room. Megan rose and drew the curtains closed. I tried not to feel out of place, but I wasn't accustomed to seeing living humans in her exalted position, and I hadn't quite found my bearings in trying to relate to her. At least Megan didn't seem disturbed by our arrival, although she'd clearly been startled when we introduced ourselves.

Cody was studying her carefully, and his face revealed some degree of interest. Normally when he scanned a person it was with an unreadable look. But then, Megan was not a suspect in anything, and this was hardly a criminal investigation. Maya was scanning her clothes, her makeup and her attitude. She hadn't made up her mind about this trainee-level goddess.

"You're wondering about the lighting," Megan said softly to Cody, as she sat down again at the far end of the sofa. She didn't seem put off by his size.

"You're right. We haven't seen any. It's only been oil lamps."

"Mazintla doesn't have any electric power any-more. Overhead, the lines are mostly still up, but twenty years ago, not long after the Zapatista revolt began, the government cut the power to this town and a number of others in Chiapas as well. A few people here have gasoline generators, but it's hard to get enough fuel in to run them, so they're used only for emergencies. I'm sure you saw what the road was like coming in. Gasoline only arrives here in cans, and most people can't afford it."

"Then there's no Internet, either," Maya said.

"Right, and this whole area is also a dead spot for phone transmissions. So no cells work here, and of course the land lines quit operating when the electricity stopped. I always talk to the people one on one before we start the service, and you wouldn't believe the hardship stories they have."

"Now we know why you didn't contact your parents after you left San Cristobal." She hadn't offered a way back into this topic, but it was time for me to reintroduce the reason for our visit.

Megan nodded. "Sure, whatever. That was the simple reason, anyway. The isolated situation here just made it easier to not think about it."

Maya leaned over the coffee table and handed her the sealed envelope from the Andersons. "We brought this for you." Megan briefly glanced at the front, and then, without opening it or showing any surprise, held one corner to the flame of the oil lamp before her on the coffee table. When it caught, she rotated it to ignite three sides, and then dropped it onto the grate in the cold fireplace nearby. It burned for a while as we watched in silence. It felt like she had just made a commentary on a long string of family conflicts that were now beyond any resolution other than this. Although coming in we hadn't suggested we had a message for her, this move almost looked planned on her part. It was like observing a well-rehearsed ritual where no response was expected, or even possible. The ceremony was too private and personal. I had the sudden thought that the Andersons may have sent another crew after her in the past. Was it one that didn't make it out of Mazintla? I wondered if this scene was both more sinister and more familiar than we thought.

"Is there another way into this town?" said Cody after a long moment. I knew he was really thinking about a second route of escape.

When the flame died in the fireplace Megan smiled as if she had fulfilled a promise to herself. Only then did she answer. "Yes, on the other side of town we have a footbridge about a hundred meters long suspended on two steel cables. It's the kind that swings back and forth as you walk on it, which is not very comfortable, and the valley bottom below is more than 800 meters down. Standing on it makes you sick to think about where you are. Naturally, no cars can ever use it. Nobody can even bring a burro across on it. It's only about two meters wide and the walkway is made of weathered wooden planks— pine, of course, so they don't last long. In the half-inch or so space between them you can see forever under your feet. It would be perfect for a scary chase scene out of Indiana Jones. Still, you would be surprised at all the things that come in here on people's backs. It brings in a lot of cheap liquor, for example. That's the main entertainment here. It's drinking, fighting, and screaming into the darkness late at night. The men sit on the edges of the slopes and listen to the echoes calling back to them. I think it makes them feel like there's someone out there that cares."

"Maybe that's your job too," Cody said, after a

long silence. Megan looked at him as if this insight was huge.

"What's at the other end of that bridge?" Maya asked. "The one on the cables."

"Only a little town called Quexil that is half a kilometer from the other end, but it's 165 kilometers away by car. It's about half the size of Mazintla."

"And six hundred meters away on foot? How did you get in here?" I said.

"By the road, like you did, but on a motorcycle. We didn't need the planks."

Of course. The narrow spot on that dirt track would not have been a problem to a vehicle with a track only one wheel wide and a driver with the kind of blinders you got from being on a mission to find God.

"I'm sorry I don't have anything to offer you to drink, but this job doesn't pay much. Nobody has any money here. Of course, I don't drink anymore myself."

"Tell me about the baby," Maya said softly. "I don't suppose your parents know about it."

While Megan's face had released its golden goddess look when we came in, now it took on an appearance that was at once sadder and more uplifting. She placed both hands over the mound of her abdomen. "No, they don't, and I don't know whether it's a boy or a girl. I haven't had any access to ultrasound here. The sad part is that it's Leo Cochrane's child and he's been dead for six weeks now. It'll be six weeks tomorrow."

I didn't fail to notice how quickly she'd shifted the discussion away from her parents. I had learned from Cody that launching people on subjects they didn't wish to discuss often led to revelations designed to distract the questioner in a different direction. Sometimes the results were more enlightening than the original answer would've been.

"Then someone told me a week later," she added, "that another person had disappeared in similar circumstances early last year. A guy Brother Nathan thought might be a rival." Her face didn't suggest how much risk she saw in this for herself.

"Your parents told us Leo came down here with you," said Cody, using his fair-minded cop expression, one that offered no surprise at statements like this. "How did he die?"

As her shoulders slumped, Megan gave him a long look, then rose from the end of the sofa and slid in next to him, her shoulder touching his arm. Her face started to crumple but she regained control of it again.

"Leo was killed by Brother Nathan's followers, the church we broke off from. I didn't see it happen but I know that's true. Leo wouldn't have left me otherwise, the way things were here. This venture with our own church was really getting some momentum when that happened. I know that's probably *why* it happened." Staring off into one of the far corners of the room that was lost in darkness, she lifted Cody's big right hand in both of hers and then looked into his eyes. "Is this all right? I get a little scared sometimes, mainly at night. I can feel it coming on again now." She held it like a teddy bear, kneading his fingers.

He smiled and nodded. "It's fine. Don't worry about it, Megan."

"I love seeing somebody from home, though. This has gotten too real."

"We all live here in México," Maya said. "This is home to us."

"And Brother Nathan is still the leader of the other congregation?" I said, finding at the last second a word other than *sect* or *cult* to use. I didn't understand the dynamic of what I was seeing between Cody and Megan, but I wanted to keep the narrative going. We could all play different roles as a case might demand.

"That's right. He's ruthless."

"Can you tell us how this breakup occurred?" I said. "Didn't you come down here thinking to join Brother Nathan's group?"

"That's what I told my parents, and that was Leo's idea. He was the religious one way more than I was. My only reason to join was so I could observe it first hand. My own background is in anthropology, but that doesn't only mean ancient cultures. I wanted to see how a modern group like this is structured, what kind of person joins it, and what the leader is like. How decisions are made and how it rewards people for staying. Is there some closely structured hierarchy, like with Scientology? And especially—and this has gotten to be a huge issue when we never meant it to be—how the group reacts when people leave."

"But to you Leo was more than a convert to a religious sect you wanted to study," said Maya.

"Well, yes, as you can see now. At first I didn't mean to get involved with him like that, but it just happened one night after a party when we were still in Minneapolis, and then it happened a lot after that. Leo was so religious he was still a virgin at twenty-five and suddenly he couldn't get enough of it." Megan paused as if looking back on events of a time long past. "When he disappeared I was still trying to decide how I felt about him. It was fun, but I didn't know how it would work for the longer term. When we were together he always came on like he was really solid, but in my experience of men that often means the opposite. Anyway, I realize this isn't a great place to have a baby, but I'm kind of settled in here now." She paused for a long moment as her lips leveled out into a thin line. "To tell you the truth, I guess I really don't know what else to do. Even before Leo disappeared, this situation had started to take off in ways I couldn't have predicted."

"What exactly happened to Leo?" said Cody. "Did you hear anything at all?" His free left hand twitched reflexively as if to pull out a pen and notebook, but he pulled it back in time.

"One of my own group here told me Nathan's followers picked him up on the street. They knew he used to go out and jog early in the morning, like before dawn. Two men locked arms with him and I never heard any more. I assume he was dropped into the valley somewhere. It's a long way down in every direction. I never saw his motorcycle again, but they would've kept that and hidden it. They're really valuable here because of how the road is."

"Did you go to the headman about it?"

She looked at Cody not critically, but with an expression that suggested he didn't realize how things went here. "The headman is a Zapatista named Rodrigo. He's not in the Brother Nathan cult but they pay him a stipend and they officially support him in what they tell the members."

"What was their problem with Leo?" said Maya.

"Within days he decided Bother Nathan was a fraud and it didn't take him long to start saying so. Nathan is just a dude from New York who thinks these people are all rubes. Like they don't have anything going on and they need some hope. That's what he's selling, but it comes with a lot of control. He has a Ph.D. in psychology, and he's really good at figuring out people's needs. At least he always says the right thing."

"But as a scam there can't be a lot of money in this for him," I said.

Megan shook her head. "No, but he's a control freak and that's what he gets out of it. You wouldn't believe all the rules that he's laid on people. Anyway, I heard he has some family money and he can do what he wants."

I said nothing about the obvious trust fund parallel there.

"Is Nathan abusing the young women in the group?" said Maya.

"Of course."

"And he wanted you too," Cody said in a softer tone.

"Yes, and do I look that available? Like I would jump into bed with him just because he was the leader? Of course, I wasn't as big then. We weren't even here a week before Leo decided we could do better on our own."

Beyond Nathan's interest in Megan, this made me wonder if Leo was also a control freak and that was part of what got him killed.

"And how was that?" I said. "What does doing better mean? Wouldn't anything be better?"

"It all started when I got my hair done like the

local women, maybe three days after we arrived. While it wouldn't work in Edina, I thought it was a cool look, and it was a way of paying tribute to the lifestyle here, saying I respected it, and I wasn't going to be aloof. I found the people very likeable. Soon the traditional hair began to get me a lot of attention. People weren't used to seeing real blondes in a remote area like this, and to have one that wanted to relate to them was shocking."

"And from there you got this church? Wasn't that a big leap?" said Maya. To my ear, her normal anticlerical tone was starting to emerge, but Megan didn't seem to notice.

"It really was. Leo started organizing some small meetings where I would talk about a different kind of religion that stressed love instead of control. Where you could be tolerant of what other people did. That was just an experiment in breaking the old patterns I had learned about in anthropology. Where Nathan was using expulsion as a punishment, I talked about not having a lot of rules or hierarchies, and instead people could do the things that made them happy if they tried to make other people happy too. We didn't plan to start this heresy, exactly, if that's even what it is, but we thought people in Brother Nathan's group were being oppressed. Gradually I began to see how a religion could be structured to be rewarding to people other than just the clergy that ran it. It wasn't about theology; it more or less just happened."

She paused for a moment, as if she hadn't ever analyzed the development of this religion that far before.

"We didn't have any theology or moralistic rules, really. We still don't. We have some music and some dancing, some flowers and incense that we mostly borrowed from Brother Nathan's ceremony because that's what people were used to and they enjoyed it. A lot of families can still do their candle ring rituals on the floor, which is an old Mayan thing. Everybody already knows the traditional Tzotzil chants, which are also Mayan in origin. So most of what we were selling was already familiar, except for the easy rules and the ideas. I know I shouldn't keep saying *we*." She paused for a moment, looking at the darkened front window. "I always try to tell a small story, like a parable, to set the tone of the service, you know? Then I do end up saying what I really believe, even if they don't always understand it all. I guess that's no different from any other religion. I just try to make it more personal and less of a formula."

"And that was where the anthropology came in," said Cody.

"Right. I tell people they can be themselves without feeling like they're evil, because we're not evil, most of us. What I say to them isn't ever coercive."

"I like it." I would've taken her hand in support of all this if Megan hadn't been already clutching Cody like he was her personal means to salvation. I had been expecting a lot more mumbo jumbo and she was refreshingly down to earth. She gave me a faint smile with a trace of weariness in it. Clearly she felt grateful to not have to be on all the time. I had felt she was unwinding ever since her fourth or fifth sentence. Who else did she have around her that she could speak with so freely, now that Leo was gone?

"So then it didn't take long for these ideas to travel through the original group like a kind of subversive wind, and soon little cliques were having secret meetings on their own, without me or Leo." Her arms lifted in a gesture without releasing Cody's hand. "I began to realize that telling the truth wasn't much different from telling a lie, if it had the same appeal to the listener. People would clutch at the right statement, the one that suited them best. The main difference was my own sense of responsibility to what I believed."

"But then it got ugly," Cody said.

"When Nathan found out what was going on he would push them out of the group right away, which turned out to be a mistake, because his numbers began to drop rapidly. Even from the first day when we arrived and came to his meeting I could already see some restlessness around me. It didn't all start with our arrival, since the seeds were already there."

A firm knock sounded at the side door. Megan

rose and opened a small view panel at head height. I couldn't hear what she said, but it was brief and authoritative, and she quickly returned alone. She leaned in against Cody as if he was her sole support, and he gave her a welcoming look. There had been times of crisis in the Agency when Maya and I had also felt reassured from just leaning against his palpable solidity.

"Soon some of them came to Leo and asked him if I would start to hold a few open meetings to let more people hear the sense of this new message. At first I wasn't wild about getting so formal with it, but Leo really liked the idea, and then I started to see how I could apply what I knew about group behavior in a culture, and that's how it went. I felt for the first time that I might have some power to change things here, which I had never thought before. I mean, nobody could be more of an outsider than I was. But then so was Brother Nathan when he started. I guess it was mostly about giving people something they could live with better, or more easily, I don't know. It all happened very quickly and without a lot of planning, kind of like this little person." She pointed at her abdomen.

"And that outfit with the breast plates was part of that?" said Maya, pokerfaced.

Megan smiled. "Well, yes, it went along with it perfectly. I already had the local hairdo, and the women had used these woven plates as part of their costume here since forever, so I thought they could be combined with a little skin. People like some skin, don't you think? Especially if it's pale and theirs is all darker. To tell you the truth, the day I got that idea, I was thinking about all the afternoons I'd spent in my bikini at the Edina Country Club pool. Skin was really important there too. I wonder if I'll ever get back into that again."

"What?" I said, "The country club?" I was startled that it still could matter in Mazintla, which seemed a world away from that lifestyle.

"No, the bikini. Fertility is always part of any religion and being pregnant helped to make me relatable. Very quickly it developed a life of its own. Then they took a vote and the majority of the group decided to split off from Brother Nathan and keep this old church for themselves. They invited me to be the pastor, or whatever. I really don't like that term, since I don't *feel* like anybody's pastor. The remainder of the original group threw together a new informal chapel down the slope a bit. It's the place with the shiny corrugated roof. Maybe you've seen it."

"I notice you've got a lot of security now," said Cody.

She nodded thoughtfully. "People thought we needed it after Leo disappeared. At this point I think I probably can't leave here by myself anymore. I have a woman who does my shopping and cleans for me. If I didn't have some money of my own I couldn't make it. I brought a fair amount of pesos in cash with me from San Cris. There's a marvelous ATM there that doesn't ask why you want it, unlike my dad."

"How can you get any more now? I mean with no Internet or phone?" I said.

"I know. I don't think I can hold on here much longer if it gets down to only what the church brings in. A lot of it is in kind rather than in cash, like goods not even in the collection plate but outside the door sometimes, where I actually turned down a small pig one morning. He was just the cutest thing! I had to say I was a vegetarian in order to not offend anyone, since he was too noisy to keep as a pet."

"Are you feeling isolated here because of the Internet being unavailable?" Maya said.

"A bit, but I'm not interested in getting back in contact with my dad. On the other hand, I'm really glad you folks showed up; it kind of brings things back to earth again. Leo always said that people saw something spiritual in me, but I never could understand what it was. Not that I don't know a few parlor tricks that look spiritual, but I'm not really a religious person, and sometimes things just develop their own momentum…"

I wondered what she meant by parlor tricks that looked spiritual. We would probably find out before this was finished.

Megan paused and placed her hand over her mouth for a moment, and when she spoke again her voice was hoarse. "But I just can't fake this anymore, you know? What it should be is the real thing, for everybody here, and that's more than I can do sometimes. Their needs are so naked. I just don't have enough resources to bring to this."

Cody patted her two gripping hands with his free one. "That's us," he said. "We're here to be the real thing, all of us. Do you think it might be time to wrap this up? We can take you back, if not to Minnesota, then to San Cristobal or San Miguel and you'll be better able to decide what to do." The Minnesota destination was only based on the Andersons' idea of how dangerous it was to live in México; not a prejudice we shared.

Megan didn't answer. There was no need to read her mind to know she was thinking about her responsibility to her congregation. If she fled Mazintla, she wouldn't even be able to say goodbye personally because word would reach Nathan immediately. What he might do as soon as she was beyond the protection of her congregation was unclear.

As we left ten minutes later Megan hugged each of us, but clung for a longer moment to Cody. We had arrived at a vague understanding that we would speak to her again the following day, after she'd had time to think through her position. She had never imagined that anyone would show up searching for her, even that she might ever be able to leave Mazintla alive. We understood the time constraint of lining all this up with Díaz' departure, but it was a big move for Megan and we didn't want to pressure her, even though, after Leo's death, it looked like the most dangerous option was for her to stay.

As we walked out into the night I was wondering what other talents she had to lure her congregation away from Brother Nathan. Her new creed had the benefit of being clean and simple. It was easy to see it as an obvious choice for people abused by fate and by their isolation. I had watched her carefully as she told her story, looking for signs of charisma, of divine fire or even just some extraordinary spark. I had seen none, yet my base instinct was that there had to be more to Megan's motives, and particularly to her skills.

With her face framed in the security door, we left the rectory and returned to the front of the church. Only one guard lingered in the flickering glow of six oil lamps on the front step, and he seemed mainly there to watch the property. Some additional light came from the rays of a half moon that traveled diagonally across the sky through streamers of ragged clouds. This time the guard had no problem letting us go inside. The four paired inner doors stood open. I can't say I had any expectations, but the interior was still surprising.

The breakaway congregation was using no

seating of any kind. The polished stone tile floor was slippery from its covering of long pine needles from the trees that grew everywhere on these slopes. In seven or eight places a ring about two and a half meters in diameter was cleared and a candle stood upright in the center. The scent of hot wax still hung in the air. A row of oil lamps marched to the front altar along both sides. From a small lantern in the roof a pair of pale angular moonbeams traced lengthened ovals on the floor that came and went in shadowy figures. Few people were present and only two of the candle circles were lit and occupied. I couldn't help thinking immediately of the fire hazard.

Maya was creeping along beside me with the vulnerability of someone wearing ballet slippers in a minefield.

"It's OK," I whispered softly. "It's the old time religion stuff, mostly from before Cortés, but with Megan as the new earth mother." Normally Maya only ranted against the Catholic Church in México.

"It's unnerving. If anything, this is worse."

"Why? Because it has indigenous roots?" Maya and I had had a conversation a while back about how much native blood she had. I got her to admit she might be as much as two percent Aztec. That was as far as she would go. Mixed blood had not been fashionable in her upper class upbringing in Mexico City, although it was not uncommon in small doses.

"Look at how much they've borrowed." She shook her head and held out her hands to encompass both walls, where tall glass-front cabinets held life-size statues of the traditional saints, but around their necks hung shards of mirror on fine chains. Their costumes appeared to be altered in every case, made to be more elaborate or ceremonial, like those of the Three Kings. It resembled a procession of alien dead, a group that had its own secret message and arcane language, one that had broken ranks with its long-time tradition and reassembled here in an unpredictable place. About a third of the way toward the front a man lay unconscious on his back near one of those saints' cabinets. Cody bent over and felt his wrist for a time.

"His pulse is normal," he said as we moved forward. All was deadly silent but for a murmur near the communion rail, where a young woman also lay on her back on the pine needles, which were clutching at her hair. She was wearing a white loose fitting top and white jeans that may have had some ceremonial meaning. White was not a color we'd seen local people wearing on the streets of Mazintla, only on Megan's skirt. Kneeling at the woman's side a shaman muttered an incantation as he passed an egg over her limbs and torso, pausing to roll it under his palm in circles on her joints. Nearby waited a glass and a bottle of soda. I knew this was for the belch at the end of the ceremony that would signal the expulsion of the evil spirit that had been harassing her soul.

Both in the spicy residue of incense that hung in the air and in the way she clung to my wrist I could sense the continuing discomfort in Maya's mind, where incense had always personified religious ritual, and she wouldn't tolerate any in our house. To her this was foreign territory to an extreme degree.

The altar at the back was densely covered with flowers, and lacked any central focus. The tabernacle in the middle had either been removed or was totally obscured. At the left stood a plain painted wooden pulpit without religious symbols, Megan's platform for her message of relaxed and humane virtue. Of course there could be no microphone, so the demands on her voice were substantial. We hadn't asked her directly if she even believed in God, but for her gentle noninvasive message, it didn't seem like she needed to.

We left in a gloomy silence, none of us finding this setting remotely uplifting. I felt like I had glimpsed a phenomenon at once both older than Christianity and newer. Was the process of religious evolution no more than the fusion we had witnessed? Was Megan Anderson's message, carried on the voice of Jalanme'tik ta Banomil, only the next genetic mutation in a long process of similar mutations, where each had been hailed as the truth, as the divine word? She had told us of her reluctant recruitment into the sanctuary. Perhaps that was not atypical for religious leaders. They are often called by a higher power, in this case popular demand.

Within this twisted orthodoxy even her bizarre costume was no more out of place than the therapeutic egg or the Coke bottle of release.

CHAPTER NINE

We need to know what the other side can bring against us before we take this any further," said Cody. It was the morning following our meeting with Megan Anderson and we had carried three of the plastic chairs out to the chilly weed-choked courtyard for this conversation. We'd all slept later than we expected, although Cody was somewhat stiff, claiming he was bent in places he hadn't ought to be.

"I thought it was clear last night that Megan sees the end coming," said Maya.

"And getting closer to delivering her baby is making her safe exit more difficult day by day," I said, "since now we have nothing like easy conditions anyway. Artemio Díaz's departure is coming up fast: the day after tomorrow in the morning, forty-eight hours."

Garrett Anderson was not going to be happy to discover his daughter wanted nothing to do with him anymore, but it was not a position we could change. Regardless of what our agreement specified about whether we had to physically deliver Megan to his door-step, put her on a plane for the far north, or simply tell him where we'd last seen her, it was certain that he was going to feel cheated by the absence of reconciliation.

Before we left her the night before, Cody had tak-en a photo of Maya and me flanking Megan on the sofa, just to prove we'd found her, and in the end that might be all of her we could ever deliver to the Andersons. If Megan wouldn't leave we would probably never know what happened to her, since this situation looked far from stable. In the photo we'd taken, her hair and eye makeup would confirm that she was off on a different tangent than Edina could provide on its wildest weekend, even during football season. Cody had been careful to frame the shot to end above her distended abdomen.

It was no surprise to any of us that the reality of Megan's situation had completely reshaped our agenda. Cases often took on their own life unconnected to our opening strategy. The game was always changing.

There was no sneaky way to approach the new tabernacle of the old cult, since we didn't have Artemio Díaz' Land Rover or anything else for a vehicle to shelter us from view, not that it wouldn't stand out on its own. Any car or truck with enough gas to move would. Loiter-ing in the street, Cody and I would look like nothing but what we were, a couple of gringos who didn't belong in this town and were likely up to no good. At least we were armed and experienced. There would be no Leo-style street abductions awaiting us.

We decided to wait until nightfall to approach the new building. For that we planned to leave Maya back at the hammock haven in case any shooting started. With her trim build, sophisticated good looks, and two or three inches of extra height over most Mexican women, there was no way to make her look like anything other than an upscale business class woman from Mexico City. She couldn't help it. Any serious attempt to disguise her would have to include that impossible local hairdo. In the meantime it was still morning, and the three of us left our dodgy lodging and trekked through town to the other end to check out the suspension bridge as a means of escape if the Díaz option should fail.

Mazintla was nondescript in the way that poverty often presents itself identically in widely separated places. Grace, charm, and cleanliness were luxuries beyond reach. Trash in the streets, stucco dropping off the walls in sheets, and rusting cars up on blocks, all make for a low cost but consistent ambience. We passed block after block of dingy one-story buildings. Most were rough red brick, oozing old and dirty mortar, although some showed signs of having once been coated with stucco and painted. Dogs and turkeys scraped and pecked the minutest patches of soil for a morsel of anything to eat. Pigs eyed us from the shadows. Soon we started comparing notes on the previous evening's encounter with Megan Anderson. I knew Maya had something on her mind.

"Standing there wearing that transparent skirt in front of all those people in that church," she said, shaking her head. "No Mexican woman would ever do that. She doesn't care about simple modesty."

I looked at her for a moment. Maya was certainly no prude. "Do you happen to recall that you have posed nude for about forty of my paintings that are now dispersed all over the map between Calgary and Quito?"

She straightened her shoulders with a huffy look. "That's not the same thing at all. Posing nude in a serious painting is an ancient and honorable tradition. Standing at a church podium where people can see your underwear is immoral, whether you are pretending to be a goddess or not. Underwear is underwear. I would never pose in my underwear. Megan Anderson is no goddess and she knows it."

I struggled with the idea that being nude might be more modest that being dressed in your underwear. "You don't think she might have copied it from someone?"

She shook her head. "That is the kind of idea she came to by her own."

And skin is skin, a universal language, I thought, deciding to write this skirmish off. Some arguments are unwinnable, no matter how logical your position. This was undoubtedly some Mexican cultural thing where the nuance of it was beyond me, even after living in San Miguel for seventeen years. What was also clear was that Maya was never going to be a fan of Megan's. She had already suggested privately to me that Megan had a rather haphazard way of getting into things, including her pregnancy, and a woman ought to maintain more control and direction in her life. This was a somewhat different matter than the costume issue.

"Aside from what a Mexican woman might do or not, that's the outfit Megan chose to capture the attention of her congregation," I said after a while. "You heard her say that. She's six years younger than you are. I haven't lived in the States for a long time but I think at that age there's more of a tendency to slide into things without a lot of planning, especially when your father has been trying to force you in one direction all your life and your heart is telling you to do something else."

"Think, if you would, of how we look at things in the Agency," said Cody as we walked. "We're always trying to estimate the outcome of various actions because that's how we understand people's motives and solve cases. I agree with Paul that a lot of people Megan's age in the States are more casual about decisions and it leads them to wake up in the soup sometimes."

"Or with Leo Cochrane," she said. "I prefer to

think of it as 'Between the sword and the wall.' And that is certainly where she is now. She's lucky we showed up when we did." When neither of us responded, she went on. "I know, I know, I'm being too hard on her. I'll lighten up. We're all she has now, I guess."

At that moment we turned a corner to find ourselves at the anchor point of the suspension bridge. At a break in the fencerow of trees that edged the cliff a pair of steel I beams had been set two meters apart into a massive concrete base, and from each a thick woven cable began a downward sloping run over the precipice. Vertical cords linked to thick rope handrails that ran along each side guarded the margins from the cable to the foot path, and the footing depended on planks about six inches wide and a couple inches thick linked by lighter steel cables. Megan had said it was about a hundred meters long, but in the swirling vapor the far end simply disappeared from view less than half that distance away.

"That is a bridge too far," Cody said somberly, shaking his head and planting his feet. "Too far for me, anyway. The other end is purely speculative and I don't have that much faith left in me any more."

"No way," said Maya. "Even if Díaz leaves without us, we're not leaving town on this contraption." This was one of her new slang words.

I suppose in a 1940s movie the bridge could have

been made to look romantic and intriguing, but my vote only made it look unanimously unwanted.

CHAPTER TEN
CODY WILLIAMS

Cody slowly crossed the plaza in the direction of Megan's church at about eleven o'clock later that same morning. He was in a reflective mood. The image of the bridge too far had remained with him all through the walk back to the hammock heaven, but what he'd failed to mention to Paul and Maya was that in his mind he had seen Megan struggling to cross it. He was even faintly troubled at his reluctance to share it with them. Her back was bare as when he first saw her, and her filmy skirt was whipping against her legs in the breeze. One hand clung to the rope railing and she did not look back as the bridge swayed from side to side. While he stared, her receding figure was absorbed by the swirling mist, still taking one tentative step at a time, as she braced herself against the lateral movement of the bridge.

Now he was glad Paul and Maya weren't with him. He needed to think about what this meant, not the image itself but the fact that it had bloomed uninvited in his mind. He had not been thinking about Megan as they approached the bridge. Cody was a levelheaded investigator who was not given to hallucination or fantasy, but the message was clear. For Megan to remain in Mazintla much longer meant she would fall into the hands of Nathan. She and her unborn child would join Leo in the ever-beckoning abyss surrounding the town.

Although he had thought often about it through an uncomfortable night in his unaccustomed hammock, he couldn't quite see what Megan wanted from him. He'd been startled when she suddenly settled in next to him and seized his hand. It seemed to suddenly break through normal physical boundaries at a time when he had only just met her. He hadn't fathered any children in the twenty-six years he was married, and he'd never before spent any time with a pregnant woman. Megan seemed at once warm and attractive, yet blousy and disheveled at the same time. He sensed that she was not in full control either of herself or the way she looked. He couldn't estimate how emotional she normally was, but her isolation and entrapment in Mazintla was enough to justify whatever she was feeling now. It was possible that her pregnancy made her more needy than she would ordinarily be. If that were true it made perfect sense to him.

Her condition also made her seem more vulnerable to a hostile move by Nathan's pious thugs, although he wasn't certain how much she consciously felt that yet. This raised his awareness of the task the Agency had taken on. He would not allow any harm to come to her on his watch, and he would do the right thing for her by his own lights, whether her father agreed with it or not. Cody realized that his awareness of her physical presence had been heightened. He had even found himself trying to study the pores in her face by the dim light of the oil lamps, as if they revealed something, and to examine her hands, which were graceful, her fingers long and tapered. Her lips looked a bit dry, odd for this climate, and her eyelashes were exceptionally long, as if she were wearing false ones, which he did not believe. He was excited to see her today without the fierce black eye makeup. As for her spirituality, he'd been able to sense nothing about it in her statements when they spoke the evening before, but in his mind he didn't automatically link it with theology. She might be the kind of person who saw all nature and humanity as one and had no need for a supernatural being to explain it.

Because of his obvious connection with Megan, Paul and Maya had both suggested that Cody be the one to take this meeting today, and he was filled with curiosity about how she would receive him. As he approached the side door of the parish house a thickset man sitting on a bench near the church façade joined him.

"You have business with the priestess today,

señor?" Cody was not surprised.

"Yes, I am thinking about joining her congregation. I have heard wonderful things about it. She is expecting me."

The man merely nodded as they paused at the door, waiting next to him. Cody rang the bell. Nothing happened. He rang it again. The man rapped on the door sharply. "No power," he said with a shrug. "The bell does not ring." In his eagerness for this meeting Cody had forgotten that.

When Megan opened the view window and nodded, the guard walked away. Cody didn't think much of his skills since he was carrying a .38 revolver under his shirt that the man had never looked for. One more reason to get Megan out of Mazintla. The appearance of security only went so far in discouraging an attack.

Once he came through the door she stared at him for a moment with a clear expression in her large eyes, as if reassessing their connection. Then she hugged him closely. Her peculiar hairdo meant she couldn't press her cheek to his neck, only her face. "I know we have some business to take care of, but just hold on to me for a minute, OK?"

Cody happily folded her in his arms. Megan was wearing the same rumpled blue skirt and sweatshirt as on the previous evening. He had nine inches of height on her and over her head he surveyed the room in daylight as he felt her soft breath on his neck.

Two barred windows at the front flanking the main entry were draped in lightweight fabric that remained drawn, although the hesitant light passed through them easily. The windows on the side facing the church were uncovered. These would be under the surveillance of the security man.

Megan pulled away. "Can I make you some tea? That's about all I have. Brother Nathan left it behind when he moved out."

Cody found it difficult to imagine Nathan living there, not that Megan was a better fit. "Sure. That would be great." He hadn't drunk a cup of tea in forty years and couldn't remember how it tasted. She seized his hand as if he were a girlfriend her same age and drew him into the kitchen. There the light was even dimmer. The stove was a curious old white and black enameled edition, now more suitable for a collector than a cook. Had there been a refrigerator it would only have been another cabinet. On the green tile counter a gas ring was linked to a small tank the size that would fit in a camper or a barbecue. She put a pot of water on with her back to him. If he had seen how she lit the flame he would've been startled.

"I suppose all the drinking water has to be carried in," he said, wishing he could read her better as she moved about. He couldn't help being tempted to see her as the daughter he'd never had. While he wanted to put that thought aside, almost as a cliché, he also wondered whether she hadn't intuited this about him at their first meeting. From his psychology training he knew about the latent sexual element in many father daughter relationships, and seeing random traces of that in her behavior toward him made Cody wonder what threads of it might have been part of her connection with Garrett Anderson. It wouldn't be incompatible with his domineering, controlling attitudes.

"Sadly. Some people can't afford to bring clean water in. I guess the wells aren't too bad if you're used to them, although they need to be awfully deep, which is another expense. No more can be drilled because they can't get the equipment in here anymore. The road coming in used to be wider years ago. Some people are saying that soon it'll be gone entirely. Mazintla will become even more isolated. The government would never help. It's bad enough already just trying to get in here."

She faced him in silence for a while, leaning against the antique tile counter, while he was seated at a small table of unfinished pine. They regarded each other comfortably.

"I don't get many people visiting who aren't swamped by problems of their own. This is fun."

"This time you're the one with a problem."

Megan put both hands to the lower edges of her

hair and scratched, as if the arrangement was too tight.

"I suppose I really do have to go, don't I, Cody? I've been thinking about it a lot. I hardly slept." She folded her arms and glanced at the pot on the burner, which was not yet doing anything.

"I want to take you out of here, Megan. I know your congregation will miss you. You must feel strongly obligated to them, especially since they broke away to be with you. But I feel you're very much at risk here. I don't have to remind you of what happened to Leo, but I will. Still, it may not be so bad. Don't you think Nathan would be relieved if you simply left quietly? You must be his biggest problem right now."

She shook her head slowly. "No. I know him. Sure, he'll be happy to see me gone, but it won't stop there. Brother Nathan will take it as an insult that I got off unpunished after pulling away half his congregation. For disrespecting his message of salvation through blind submission, he'll come after me, if not in person, then he'll send some of his security people. He identifies with the God of the Old Testament. I hate to admit it, but I'm not comfortable here anymore. I think it's going to catch up with me in some way, not as bad as it did with Leo, perhaps, but you never know. If I left and he pulled his congregation together again, he'd have a stronger base from which to come after me. The most dangerous time would be when I'm between here and the highway."

Cody made an expansive gesture with both hands. "But you have me. You can depend on me and the Zacher Agency. This is not the toughest situation we've ever been in by a long shot, and Paul and Maya are no lightweights, either of them. All three of us have killed people that came up against us in the past, Megan. I don't say that to brag, only to indicate that we can and will go the distance if necessary. Nathan can't bring anything against us that we haven't seen more than once before, and several times as big as he could ever be, no matter who he thinks he is or which god is on his side."

A broad smile lit her face. "I know. You're the big guy. You make me feel like I don't have to be scared anymore. I think the reason I hate to admit it is that it underlines how much I depended on Leo, which I tried not to believe at the time. I never realized it—and this is going to sound ugly—until he was gone and I felt like he had let me down. Isn't it awful to say that?"

"It's awful and it's natural at the same time. But I care about you. I'm happy to admit it, and I'll see you through this." A strange feeling, almost a shiver, swept through Cody's limbs, as if she might misinterpret this. In his own mind he was very clear about how he meant it. Megan was a young woman in a tough spot who needed a father's help, the kind of father who was not about to put up with anything.

She turned and walked to the window. "All the same, though, I don't feel that Maya likes me very much. That's what I picked up last night from her look and from the tone of her conversation."

"What you may have sensed is that she's protective of her relationship with Paul, and she's like that with any young attractive woman. But don't think for a moment that she wouldn't come out shooting if you were threatened. She's as tough as any of us."

"How old is she now?"

"Thirty."

"She still looks pretty good. I also think she has a thing for you." Folding her arms, Megan gave him a level glance.

Of all the directions this conversation might take, this was far from the one Cody was most comfortable with. His mouth opened and closed twice before he answered. "But that's not exactly the way it is."

Megan looked at him again, but at that moment the water came to a boil and she turned to brew the tea with a reflective expression. "I'm sorry I don't have any milk or sugar."

"That's OK."

"Then I must have it backwards, don't I? It's you that's hot for her." She set down a mug in front of him, but didn't move back to the counter as she waited for a response.

Cody rubbed his face with both hands. Why was this so difficult to talk about with her?

"Yes."

"Yes what?"

"I always wanted to be the one with Maya. She knows that and so does Paul. It's only something that's been out there for a long time, and she even kids me about it now and then. Sometimes she tempts me, humorously, I guess. It's not like it's a problem inside the Agency."

"Isn't it, though? If the bullets were flying, who would you protect first?"

Of course Cody knew it would come to this—it had always been the bottom line. "If I could only protect one person, it would be Maya. I couldn't live with myself if anything happened to her." Cody took a careful sip of his tea. With a greenish amber cast, it tasted slightly astringent. He didn't mind it. "Where is this going?"

"I just want to know where I stand if we leave Mazintla. I have a support group here, shaky as it is. I know that Pablo outside is loyal, even though he isn't all that good, but part of what keeps Nathan from coming after me now is also my congregation. He knows they'd come down on him in droves if he tries anything. But once we leave this building or the church, then it's all on you guys in the Agency."

"We're all armed. Are you saying Nathan would

come after us on the road?"

She only nodded. "Have you ever been shot?"

"Four times, and I'm still standing."

"Then I think you'll do." She paused for a moment and her face grew more serious. "You know, I have this crazy idea. You might not like it, so tell me now if it makes you uncomfortable."

"Try me."

"I want you to be my stepdad. Do you have any kids?"

"Not until now."

CHAPTER ELEVEN

As dusk thickened into darkness that day Cody and I found ourselves prowling Mazintla without Maya, edging along the border of pines that skirted the southern side of the village. We already knew that at a break ahead, the land dropped about six meters and on a rocky promontory stood the new cult temple. It was informally built of staves for the walls and covered shed-like with a series of shiny corrugated metal roof panels. Putting it up must have stretched the slender resources of the newly divided community. Megan told us it had only a dirt floor, and of course there was no electric lighting. We lingered at the limit of the trees to watch what might develop. Stragglers were arriving over the side on a long ramp to attend a service, lit at the edges by the ever-present oil lamps. At the entrance a small crowd was waiting, many holding candles that illuminated their faces but little else. Only one man was watching the entrance, looking people over.

I wondered if Nathan traveled with his own

security. He must have been sensitive to the risk from the other side, aware that Megan's group assumed he had ordered the death of Leo Cochrane. It was an uneasy standoff. Cody and I weren't planning any moves against him, but if he was behind that murder, and possibly an earlier one, then we both felt we needed to have some idea of what he was capable of launching against Megan when she was unprotected, or even when she was.

After about ten minutes, from a shadowed street on the right, a pair of headlights drove up to the edge and stopped. My first thought was that Nathan was privileged enough to have a supply of gas. It may have been the red crew cab pickup we'd met on the road in, but I couldn't be sure in the dark. Lights went on inside and after a moment the driver opened a rear door. As it swung outward a short man got out wearing a dark monk's robe with a pointed hood. Looking down, his face remained in deep shadow. Two others with broad shoulders and about six or eight inches taller joined him one on each side and they descended the ramp.

"There's our man," said Cody.

"I'd like to bust him," I said, "but Leo's murder is not our case."

"I'll tell you one thing; if he comes after Megan, or any of us, I'll take him down myself in a heartbeat. No regrets."

After about five minutes had passed, with the

bulk of the crowd inside, the drums and music began. The melody swirled up through an alien tonality, voices that may have been speaking of a world colder than Megan's, a world where salvation could only be sought in a single narrow place bordered by the inflexible will of the leader. An eerie soprano voice wound through this rhythm in words I couldn't make out; they may have been in Tzotzil, and the tune itself older than the advent of the *conquistadores*. We slipped away in silence, grateful for the darkness around us, which gathered the village closely into its gloomy hands.

CHAPTER TWELVE

The plan for Megan's deliverance was a simple one, which was reassuring, since complicated plans only offer more ways to fail. Artemio Díaz pursued his rigid schedule, and beyond wishing us well, in his single-minded way he was not concerned with any details of our case. Cody had met briefly with him at the headman's house after he'd seen Megan and worked out the proposed details. At the hammock hostel Díaz would simply collect us with our single battered suitcase at seven o'clock in the morning of the day he left, and we would proceed without fanfare to the parish house two blocks away. Not much would be moving at that hour, or at any hour, so no real concealment in traffic was available.

Once we arrived, Megan would walk out with her backpack and get in the Land Rover. If we saw no one else in view other than her security man, none of us would exit the car. If anyone else did appear, we'd have to get out and secure the situation. We preferred not to do this because anything more than Megan simply walking across to the worn stone pavers at the edge of the parish yard would create a larger scene. Few people had a car with any gas, and when one appeared, all the dogs ran down to check it out, barking. We didn't have any dog food with us to toss out the window and distract them.

We had briefly discussed leaving before dawn, but Díaz didn't want to navigate the exit road in the dark. This made perfect sense to all of us.

It was now reassuring that no telephones were working, either landline or cell, in the village. Boys lingered near the edges of the plaza waiting to take messages at a run across town for a peso. Any news only traveled on foot, which would give us a chance to get out on the crippled link to civilization without attracting a curious group of witnesses.

No one was on the street when we left the hostel to pick up Megan, and even though I saw the shutters at the front window open just after we pulled away, I thought little of it. Our innkeeper had no power to do anything to stop us, and although we'd paid our paltry bill, he couldn't have known what we intended. During our stay we'd exchanged no more than twenty words with him.

The morning had begun like all the others: chilly with streamers of mist that trailed from a drifting gray sky. In the clenched atmosphere in the car no one had much to say. We were on edge waiting to get Megan into the back seat without incident. Her pregnancy gave her a unique limitation and we were all a little more nervous because of that, even though it was less than fifty feet from the parish house door to the rear door of the Land Rover.

When we paused at the curb between the church and the residence my watch said 7:05. We had told her seven o'clock, knowing we'd be a few minutes late. All three of us had our guns out and ready, which made Díaz a little antsy at the wheel. He may not have realized before that we were all armed.

"I know this will be OK for all of you," he said softly, more to himself than to us. "Still, I have bandages in the back."

Cody's fingers began to tap out a nervous rhythm on the windowsill, but stopped when he realized he was doing it.

I almost jumped out to fetch Megan at her door, but it was still better if she was seen leaving alone if she was observed at all. A moment later she emerged from the side of the parish house, pulling the door firmly but silently shut behind her. She didn't lock it or look around at the Land Rover, moving toward us at a normal pace staring at the pavement as if to avoid a stumble. When she was five feet away I opened the rear door to her and slid over as she lifted the backpack from her shoulders and got in. Díaz pulled away at an unhurried pace and headed toward the road out of town. I didn't notice the security man, but he must have watched her leave. Three or four dogs from the plaza ran along beside us barking their farewells.

I watched through the rear window, as I'm sure Díaz also did in his mirror, but I saw no one following us. It was about five long blocks to the narrow ridge road through the gorge. The leisurely pace was torture, but going faster on that rough dirt road would've had us bouncing off the roof of the Land Rover. I suppose doctors have learned to be more patient, but if I had been Díaz I would've still been stomping on the gas pedal.

Megan was wearing her standard rumpled blue skirt and the Edina sweatshirt. None of it was clean. I began to wonder if she owned anything else. Probably she still had some things that didn't fit her anymore and the backpack didn't offer much capacity.

"Everything OK?" said Cody from the front, reaching over the seat to grip her hand. The question was clearly meant mainly for her, but the rest of us would've answered it in a variety of ways.

"Yes, but I'm really sad to slip away like this." Her voice was heavy. "I left them a long message. It took me two hours and three different drafts to get it right. I'm still not sure it is."

As we drove over the edge of the plateau and started downward on the modest slope, no one was behind us. We all could've verified that from whatever mirror we were watching. The atmosphere on the road ahead was thick with mist and drifting vapor. In half a minute we could no longer see the nearest parts of Mazintla behind us. I wasn't sorry to leave, although it was obvious that the trip back would be slower than coming in.

In the car the silence was as thick as the atmosphere outside. Megan sat on my right with her hands folded on her lap and stared straight ahead, her lips pressed into a thin line. Maya was on my left, silent, looking out the window at nothing that possessed any shape or promise. Megan had not yet been able to decide on her final destination. For her just to agree on this exit seemed as much as could be managed for a while. At the back of everyone's mind was the critical crossing point awaiting us on the road ahead. Had this dismal track deteriorated any further? I was now looking at it as the eye of the needle. I always think of tipping points like this coming later, nearer the end of a case as kind of a release of tension, but that was far away and we all knew it. Still, Díaz seemed calm and ready for this transit from one world to another, even if the rest of us weren't. He was, of course, ignorant of the detail of Megan's story. Or was he? Díaz was no chatterbox. I decided his calmness was due to the fact that he dealt with life and death issues all the time.

A kilometer along we paused about fifteen meters ahead of the gap in the road. It looked about the same as when we'd crossed three days earlier. The silence around us was profound and almost sinister in its thick obscurity. No rain had fallen during our brief sojourn in Mazintla, so once we passed the damaged portion, the road further on would probably be much like it had been on the way in. I got out with Cody and Díaz and we started on the same double-layered diagonal repair we'd used before. I tried not to study the edges of the narrow track where we worked. With his greater weight Cody would go over first if it crumbled. The mist filling the valley below gave us the uncanny sensation of laboring above the clouds. Oddly, I could see no birds sailing past. Perhaps they needed to know where the ground was.

I found myself breathing more rapidly, as if the air had grown thinner, which it obviously hadn't. Entering didn't feel quite like this, although the supply of planks and saplings was very much as it had been then. This told me Nathan had not anticipated our flight. He could've maintained control far better by stationing a crew where we were now at the break in the road. This made me wonder whether Megan had been wrong in her comment about him. Perhaps he really did prefer to see her gone and was not going to make it more difficult to leave. Perhaps he had a streak of mercy when it was in his own interest. Perhaps.

When I looked back toward Mazintla the mist had already fully covered it. It was as completely disappeared as we were as we hovered between two invisible points, just as we had imagined we might on the suspension bridge. Maybe none of this had really happened. Once we were beyond the gap we'd belong to a different world, one somehow more anchored in reality. Almost anything would be, I thought.

But just as we finished layering the planks together, the rising whine of an accelerating motorcycle rapidly approaching made us all whirl around and peer back again toward the town. People wouldn't drive that fast on this filmy road in the clouds without being on a serious mission, and I could only think of one. We rushed back inside the Land Rover. As Díaz put it in gear the young man on the approaching motorcycle had nearly reached us. He leaped off without stopping, laid it down sliding on its side and kicking up gravel behind us as he rushed forward on foot. Staggering, disregarding us, he dashed toward the planks in a bent over posture, both arms extended. We all saw what was about to happen.

Cody pulled out his gun, but he was seated on the wrong side of the Land Rover to have a good shot. Maya seemed frozen, with her mouth open in alarm as she was just starting to grope for her weapon. All that the boy needed to do was to pull two or three of the planks towards him and the other ends would no longer rest on the far side of the gap. The Land Rover would cartwheel into the gorge with them.

Díaz stomped on the gas pedal and we bolted forward trying to launch the vehicle onto the planks before the kid could pull the other ends away. We all reached the edge at about the same instant. The kid's hands were just grasping the first two when Díaz swung the steering wheel hard to the left and immediately back. The veering front fender of the Land Rover propelled the motorcyclist off the edge. After a grim moment when the spinning tires seemed about to lose their grip on the slippery planks and send us after him, we straightened out and passed over the improvised bridge with an un-restrained shout of triumph. It did not quite mask his fading wail piercing the mist as he dropped into the abyss. The sound was abruptly cut off three seconds later.

In the more sober silence that followed, Artemio Díaz drove on at a restrained pace, shaking his head. "So now it has come down to this. We trade five lives for one," he said thoughtfully after a long moment while we climbed the slope on the other side. "I suppose he will now be a saint in their pantheon. Sad for him, being so young, but not a bad exchange for us."

Megan covered her face, no doubt imagining Leo going over the edge earlier in that same way. "I'd call it nearly six," I heard her say through her fingers. "And that was Leo's motorcycle."

"An evil man, this Nathan. The headman told me he has killed before you came, Señorita Jalanme'tik ta Banomil." We drove on in silence for a kilometer or so. It wasn't hard to imagine what anyone was thinking.

"But I'm sure you've never had to kill anyone intentionally before," said Cody in a gentle commiserating tone to Díaz. I was surprised that he said this, but then he had dealt with death his entire career.

The doctor shook his head. "Well, for me it occurs all the time. Most often they're much older, though, when they go, and they can't wait to leave their suffering behind. It's just my job, you know? That's how it has always been here."

I knew this happened, perhaps more in México than in the States, but I'd never heard it acknowledged so frankly. What followed for a long time was silence as we swayed carefully through the ruts and muddy gullies of our escape route. The dense haze still wrapped most of the landscape and streamed from the trees like a pale strain of moss.

Artemio Díaz spent his current life in a sustained effort to save people in remote areas. I wondered what he thought we'd dragged him into on his own turf. On the other hand, he operated every day in a far more difficult world than we did. Maybe it was nothing but our own self-importance that made me think we'd stressed him out, trying to pry this privileged young woman out of a situation of her own casual making, and then leaving a ruinous scene behind us. On the other hand, we could hardly have left her there. The Zacher Agency's task of providing solutions fortunately does not include offering answers or moral judgments. The job of detective philosopher was one I had never encountered and didn't care to audition for. It would've put me out of my depth.

Maya folded her arms and stared out the side window with a disgusted look. After a long moment her hand sought mine in the recess between us. I knew she was marking all this up on the scorecard of religion, one side being what it claimed to do for people, versus the woes it inflicted on them on the other. She would say the church entry was always a doorway to abuse, and being a historian, she could back that up quite well with an armload of facts.

"The rest of you will find no better answer for this," said Díaz without turning around, but clearly addressing Megan. I wondered if he had one he wasn't sharing. "I do not ask why they wanted so much to keep you there, Señorita Jalanme'tik ta Banomil. If Señor Nathan had not built serious weaknesses into his group, no one would have talked to you about leaving him. No one would've broken away. This is the error all the churches make—they build the group on the basis of their people's needs and then ignore them once it is established." She looked back at him but made no response.

I wasn't sure I agreed with this. I thought most churches traveled on their own momentum. Maya nodded in silence. I began to focus on the end of this trip, on the rational paved roads ahead, the ones without sheer drop-offs, the sunny skies, the sane and benign people, real restaurants, and being back in our comfortable van dedicated to our own purposes on our own schedule. Throughout our time in Mazintla I had always felt we were only a footnote to Díaz' larger crusade—but that was inevitable. This felt like a case that had been cobbled together from pieces left over from a failed experiment.

We'd never had a chance to ask Díaz why he hadn't told us about Megan's cult leader role at the church. It was as if he had just pointed in her direction and went on with his business. It was possible that now we never would have that chance, since he was clearly in a hurry to get on with ministering to his next group of patients, and I didn't feel we could ask that in her presence. With his knowledge of Tzotzil he had always known what Jalanme'tik ta Banomil meant. I wondered whether he didn't think it was better for us to make our own discoveries about what she was up to. He was a fixer, not a meddler, as he had suggested to Cody earlier. On his return from that conversation in the blue house Cody had given us a full report.

At half past eleven o'clock, with a collective sigh we climbed a brief slope and emerged onto the highway forty meters beyond. Díaz only offered a chuckle, but I thought I detected a note of relief in it. The morning air was still chilly but I could see patches of blue sky ahead in the direction of San Cristobal. The mist thinned as we turned south toward El Toro Verde cantina. I checked my cell, but we were still in a zone without service. Maybe at the cantina we could grab some lunch before we picked up the van and hit the road again. We'd been getting by on gorditas from the plaza and fruit from the tiny market stalls scattered here and there throughout the town. A couple of tiendas supplied bottled water and beer. We'd all been wondering how sanitary the street food was, but none of us had gotten sick. Cody may have dropped a pound or two.

Less than two kilometers after the highway turnoff we drove in alongside the cantina with a sense of relief, of coming to earth after a bizarre adventure we could enjoy reminiscing about in a quieter time, but would never have any interest in repeating. No one appeared as we pulled out our single suitcase and Megan's backpack and set them beside the Land Rover. Megan and Maya both hugged Díaz and thanked him for his assistance. Cody and I firmly shook his hand, sure that we'd never see him again.

"Now you have miles to go before you sleep,"

Megan said to him. I don't think Díaz understood the reference but he nodded anyway.

"I hope you and your child will find a new beginning," he said, taking her hands in his. I could sense a slight impatience in his eyes. He had a greater mission than our safe return, and this was the end of the road for our brief collaboration. I could feel his trust in our ability to carry on from there, his belief that he had done enough for us, and that Megan was going back in good hands. We had paid him the thousand dollars before we left San Cristobal and he had said that some of it was already invested in the medical supplies in the back of the Land Rover.

"I'm sorry it went this way," I said. "As you know, our best hope was to get out unnoticed. They must've been watching us."

"Some here would call what happened fate. This time I think I will agree. Nothing else makes any sense. *Adiós, amigos.*"

Sensing one phase, at least, of this case successfully wrapping up, we all watched him pull away and head back north with a mixture of both sadness and relief. His wave to us was equally one of farewell and of benign dismissal. He had never said what his next destination was, but no doubt it would be some small, isolated place with no hope and no medical care beyond his monthly visits. I didn't envy him, even though he was doing what he loved. For us the road was wide open and ready. We'd be having an early dinner in San Cristobal as we figured out what Megan wanted to do for her next move. Perhaps she would even decide to stay there, where some people already knew her and there was more than one decent hospital to use when her time came. As we stood there watching the Land Rover disappear over a gentle slope, I knew she was working that out herself. Cody put his hand on her shoulder and she moved a step closer to him. I realized I was still shaking my head at how it had ended for Díaz back on the gap in the road. It was always dangerous to get too close to us and we had never warned him of that, fearing that he wouldn't take us to Mazintla if he knew.

It was in that condition of relieved anticipation for all of us, of a difficult case winding down but not yet ended, that we took the suitcase and backpack and walked around to the back of the cantina to find that the van was gone.

CHAPTER THIRTEEN

I t is not necessary to repeat my initial response to the van's disappearance, since it was widely broadcast throughout the valley far below in a volume and tone of voice I hadn't realized I possessed until that moment. I had no doubt that the cantina owner had some affiliation to Brother Nathan's cult. Of course it was too late to question Díaz about the man. Pounding on both the back and front doors of El Toro Verde brought no result. The pair of steer horns mounted on each of the doorframes shook and trembled in a way they likely never had in life. The windows were all shuttered inside. At this time of day, someone should've at least been in the kitchen doing the prep work for lunch and comida. Someone should've been setting the tables. Cody stomped around the building and returned with a frustrated shrug.

"We're going in; I'm in no fucking mood to put up with this kind of bullshit. Excuse my French, Reverend Anderson," he said, pulling out his lock picks from their belt sheath.

I don't believe he ever left home without them. Megan looked at him as if this was a side of him she'd never seen before. He worked for a couple of minutes with no visible result.

"What's it like?" said Maya, studying his fingers.

"Well, it's an older lock, but this one's good quality. Better than on the front door. I'd always rather work on a decent one because you know how it's made, even if it's not been well maintained." Megan watched him in surprise mingled with admiration. Picking a lock is a delicate activity, and seeing it happen has a pace similar to that of watching ice forming.

"How are you feeling?" Maya said to Megan. "We can use the bathroom and get some food, at least. I don't think this will hold us up too long."

I was impressed by her matter-of-fact optimism. We were still hours away from San Cristobal.

"I'm just happy to be over that hump," Megan said. "We can get another vehicle somehow, can't we? That's just basic commerce. You can replace a car anytime, anywhere."

But this is not Edina, I thought to myself, although I didn't respond. Possibly if we could get to Ocosingo, sixteen kilometers down the road. At that instant from some distance away I began to hear a wail unwinding on the northerly breeze. I could sense it streaking through the filmy mist on the highway. "Listen," I said. "Do you hear that high-pitched whine, or maybe two of them combined? I do think it's two now, dividing and coming this way."

We all studied the delicate movements of Cody's hands as we listened. He seemed to be harvesting a subtle response from the lock, reading it from his fingertips, but the process couldn't be rushed.

"Motorcycles," whispered Megan, nodding slowly, even sadly. "I think one of them is Leo's, the same one we saw the kid lay down on that road back there, the one who went over the edge. I traveled on the back of that bike all the way to Mazintla, since he bought it when we got to San Cristobal, and this sounds like the same pitchy whine it always made as he went through the gears."

"Great," said Maya, "just great." She reached for her gun.

The sound was nearer now, perhaps within half a kilometer or less. Soon the pitch dropped a bit as if the riders knew where they planned to stop. My skin was prickling with anticipation. With a triumphal grunt, Cody rolled the last of the lock tumblers over and the door swung open with a twist of the knob. We all jumped inside and slammed it behind us.

"Bolt it! Bolt it!" said Maya and Megan simultaneously.

Cody shook his head with an ugly jut to his chin. He was in a mean mood and primed for a confrontation. "No, no, this is exactly what we want now," he said. "We're going to nip these clowns in the bud. Find a place to hide inside. Get down behind the bar, if there is one, and keep your gun ready, Maya. If anyone gets past us and approaches Megan, blow them away without mercy. They're walking into a trap, and Paul and I will take them down coming in. We need those bikes ourselves now. How nice that they delivered them to us."

I had been imagining four of us hitchhiking with a suitcase in tow.

Trailed by Megan, Maya ran up the four steps and disappeared toward the front, closing a door after them. I heard a bolt slide home with the solid impact of metal hitting metal. On each side of the short corridor where we waited was another door. On my side it opened into a staff restroom and on the other side a storeroom. Without relocking the outer door, Cody and I stepped inside these adjacent rooms, leaving the doors open five or six inches. The way they were situated, both opening inward, we'd be able to look around the edge and come up behind our visitors once they moved past us toward the stairs. If they found a way to get that upper door open they'd both take a bullet. Suddenly I remembered the explosive impact of gunfire in close quarters. In our second case I had shot a man inside a car and my ears kept ringing for days.

The only light came from a divided window in the transom above the outside door. No sound came from further inside the cantina where Maya and Megan must've been counting their own heartbeats. Cody and I waited in our hideaways, practically holding our breath. Mine, the restroom, stank of stale urine and a nasty disinfectant that was worse. When I took a step backward to check the cylinder of my gun I heard the subtle crunch of one of the huge local cockroaches beneath my heel. I knew we wouldn't have to wait long for the party to begin.

The next sound I heard might have been the substantial click of a kickstand near the rear door, snapping out and locking in place. It sounded overconfident to me as we waited in silence. Then the tiniest of squeaks came from the doorknob as it turned, or it may have been from been a hinge. An instant later from the change in the ambient light I could tell that the back door had opened. A whisper followed, the words too low to make out, but enough to tell us there were two men coming in. The words could have been in Tzotzil. My gun was still cold and ready in my hand. I had already cocked it before the door opened.

When the shadow crossing my doorway told me they had passed, Cody and I stepped out at the same instant, guns raised to the backs of two short men. They were both slender, not the bulky security volunteers we'd seen guarding Megan's church.

"Freeze," Cody said, in his most guttural cop tone. (He actually said, "Stop!" since commanding them in Spanish to drop rapidly in temperature would not have had the same effect as in English.) One of them instantly reached into his belt but Cody's left fist connected powerfully with the man's ear and he dropped silently onto the tile, unknowingly hitting his forehead on the bottom step. The other one didn't move until Cody's grip on his shoulder thrust him to the floor with his friend.

I frisked them both and lifted a large pocketknife from the conscious man's jeans. He had no gun. The other carried a small, well-worn revolver at the front of his belt. I stuck both in my pockets. "Maya!" I yelled, stepping over them and pounding on the door at the top of the stairs, "They're down. Can you find some rope or clothes line up there in the kitchen or laundry?"

Two minutes later the bolt slid back and Maya peered around the door, offering a coil of clothesline, two cloth napkins, and a couple of dishtowels for gags. It was no surprise that the cantina would hang its clean linens out to dry; electricity and gas are expensive. Once they were bound hand and foot we dragged both men into the restroom and closed the door. Neither side had offered any conversation.

After Megan and Maya came out with us, Cody relocked the back door. Taking the suitcase with two people each on a pair of medium-sized motorcycles was not an option, although I have seen three and even four people on one in San Miguel. One passenger of course would've been an infant. We pulled out a few critical things, stuffed them in Megan's backpack and took off in the direction of San Cristobal. The suitcase remained leaning against the north wall of El Toro Verde.

For weight distribution, we put Cody with Maya on the larger of the two, and Megan sat behind me. I could feel the thrust of the baby inside her. Her arms gripped me as if I were the future. If she felt it was strange to leave the area on Leo's bike again, she didn't bring it up. She would've had to shout over the engine noise.

Cody had ridden a Harley–Davidson with the police for a while in his early patrolman days, and I had owned an old Honda in college, so these mid-size bikes were nothing new. Between the whine of the engine and the wind, no conversation was possible until we arrived in San Cristobal at about 4:30 that afternoon. We all had a lot to think about anyway.

CHAPTER FOURTEEN

I'm sure more of them will be coming soon," said Megan in a cheerless tone, sliding carefully into a booth at The Scholar. It provided only a couple of centimeters extra clearance beyond her abdomen. "Even if Nathan hadn't planned to kill me before he will now after that kid went over the side."

We were all starving and road-weary. A sense of great relief at leaving Mazintla had somehow evaded us, although the thought of eating soon was compelling. Megan pulled off her sunglasses, which the sky had never suggested she needed, and set them on the napkin at her right. "You know they'll come after us. This was not the end of the story today. They'll scare up some more motorcycles and let those guys out of the cantina, and..." Her voice trailed off even as she made a helpless gesture. She had become fixated on it and I couldn't blame her.

"They probably have the van as well," I said.

Megan's blue cotton skirt had been uncomfortably hitched up to mid thigh so she could straddle the motorcycle seat behind me. From the knees down her legs still had a bluish cast from the chill wind. She had told us earlier that three months before, when she arrived in Mazintla, she'd had no more than her backpack and she'd given away some of her clothes before they left San Cristobal. People at two other tables leaned over and whispered something about her hairstyle without actually pointing, but their startled look was still evident.

The rest of us had our toothbrushes and our guns, a change of underwear or two, and little else, except that Maya had saved some lipstick and eyeliner. One consolation was that the hotel was storing our other suitcase. In our rush to eat we hadn't stopped to claim it yet, because the other issue, one of many now, was what we would do with it in the absence of my van.

"How will they know where to look for us?" Cody was already thumbing his way through the menu in search of a substantial meal that was not based on spinach or tofu. Since we hadn't been eating that well, I sensed he might be softening up for other options soon, moving off his starting position that in order for him to eat, something had to die.

Megan shrugged. "I don't know, but they seem to have threads everywhere. Maybe their followers are embedded in this town too, like little spies for their god, whoever that is."

"What is it that they want from you now?" asked Maya. "Maybe you don't know them well enough to say."

Megan leaned back in the booth and folded her arms. "I think they're looking for a sacrifice, or maybe an enemy to overcome. To have someone lose her life for his religion would make Nathan happy and complete. He has small tolerance for dissent. I would be a perfect example of what happens when you don't totally bow down and submit to the leader."

"So you would be like the fatted calf in that situation, rather than a martyr," Maya said, giving her a level look. With a flick of her wrist she subtly waved off the waitress, which earned her a desperate look from Cody.

Megan looked at her for a moment. "Pretty much. Being disemboweled in my condition would offer him some special significance, like doubling down in online blackjack."

"Then I think that Brother Nathan might find himself in a far more dangerous position than he realizes," said Maya. "Because in the Agency we don't ever lay down in front of anyone. If he comes after us again, Nathan will discover the pathway to his own martyrdom instead of yours."

"Amen," said Megan, picking up the menu with a determined look. "Amen in the everlasting lord, or whatever Nathan's straw man is. That part was never clear to me. He always tried to draw in some old Mayan elements to make his pitch seem more authentic. How about one of these giant frosted cinnamon buns and a side of bacon with a cheddar and onion omelet? They serve breakfast here all day. That was always my favorite."

"Sounds like a winner," said Cody. "I've become so light I'm about to float up to the ceiling." Thinking of the Hindenburg drifting untethered through the room, I tried not to imagine this in more detail.

"Don't you guys ever get tired of people trying to kill you?" Megan said after the orders went in.

"It does get old at times," said Maya. "But we all have other passions to give us some relief. I've got a horse that I'm missing now and Cody has a lot of football to watch this time of year."

"And I like to paint pictures now and then." I pulled out my cellphone and checked it. For the first time in several days I had a signal. The others got theirs out too, except for Megan.

"Mine needs a recharge. It's been dead for a long time."

"I've gotten six messages from your father in the past four days." I scanned them quickly. None were very long. "I would say that his dominant theme is mostly the same. 'Where the hell is Megan?' That's usually followed by, 'Why aren't you calling me back?' The courtesy with which they're framed deteriorates a bit more on each successive one. I think I'll respond later when we settle in for the night, wherever that is. I'm too hungry to be diplomatic right now."

It was only when the food arrived and was about halfway finished that we were able to think about other things.

"The motorcycles go back and forth a lot," said Megan between bites. A dollop of white frosting from the bun clung to the corner of her mouth, but I don't think she cared. "They probably saw your van and since it had Guanajuato plates then they figured it had to be yours. I don't think you'll see it again. Sorry. You must have thought finding me would be easier than it was. I hope my dad is paying you guys well for what you're putting up with from him too."

"Nothing is ever easy," Cody said, working on two corned beef sandwiches on rye with four dill pickle spears (rare in México) and a bowl of papaya and pineapple chunks. We were all on our second cup of coffee. Garrett Anderson's expense budget was going to take a serious hit on this meal, but then he'd gotten off for a pittance back in Mazintla. For a while I'd considered charging him for the food we should've eaten but couldn't find.

"What's their next move?" I said to Megan, not wanting to talk about her father any more, since his manner was starting to irritate me. After what we'd been through his impatience seemed self-indulgent and inappropriate.

"Did you tell anyone in Mazintla where you were staying here in San Cris?" she said. "That would be one thing. They'll also be watching the bus station, since they have your van."

"I wonder if they ever tried to bring it into Mazintla?" I said. "That might be too tough, so maybe they've got it somewhere around here."

Maya reached into her purse and lifted a set of van keys into the air. "The second set," she said. "We always travel with two."

"Unfortunately, the set they have also has our house key on it."

"Without that van we're going back home on the bus," Cody said, "and that's a very uncomfortable prospect. It's not rare for them to be highjacked down here, even if we don't have a shootout in the bus depot."

Of course, we could've flown back too, from Tuxtla Gutierrez, the capital, but to do that, we'd need to abandon our guns, which seemed suicidal after what we'd been through so far.

"Are you still comfortable about settling in San Miguel, at least for now?" Maya said to Megan. This was where we had tentatively left it in the Land Rover.

"It would give me better cover than this town ever could."

After we finished we decided to go back to the

Hotel Misión to retrieve some clean clothing from our suitcase. It was a clear late afternoon and we were too well fed to be moving very fast. The route took us past Artemio Díaz' blue house. It sits on a long block, with the street one way heading east, and as we traveled past a line of parked cars I noticed two men and a woman across the street and further down toward the end, standing at Díaz' doorstep. The woman wore the unmistakable Mazintla hairdo. Of course Díaz was not there to open the door to them, he was still on the road to his next destination of mercy, or perhaps he had already arrived there. Seeing him only as the link with us, they may not have known that.

"Well, look over there," said Cody. "That's a hairdo you will not see around this town that often." We slowed for a few paces. "And now I believe I know how they got here too."

"Either they followed us here or they think we came back with Díaz," I said.

"Right, but I'm talking about your van now, parked five cars up on our side of the street."

It was true, right down to the Guanajuato license plate and the bullet hole just above the upper left corner of the back door. I'd never had it filled and painted over because I thought it earned me a certain amount of respect when I parked the van on Quebrada as near as I could get to our house.

"You can thank me for this later," said Megan. "I have special powers of attraction."

Here come the palm frond breastplates again, I thought. I know how that works. But was there more to her game? It wasn't the moment to ask.

We all ducked and scuttled along below the profile of the parked cars and pickups. Maya unlocked the van doors and we slipped in from the sidewalk side. The three people across the street and down a bit weren't concerned with us; they appeared to be having a heated conference about what to do next.

With Maya's reserve set of keys I backed the van out without any special display of eagerness. Across the street their heads were huddled together and it was only at the last moment as we cruised quietly past that one of the men looked up and gave us a startled look of recognition. He would've seen Cody glaring at him with a triumphant grin from the passenger front seat. With a bit of bravado I hit the gas pedal and sped away.

Still, as in any recovery, we were not quite whole, of course. The sound and navigation systems had been jimmied out and the void in the center of the dash gaped with a nasty variety of twisted colored wires. My two choice Shakira CDs from the center console were gone too, although the thieves had mercifully left behind Maya's favorite, the four-CD set of Tony Bennett in his prime. Our travel roll of toilet paper was also gone from the glove compartment. This was not going to cost Garrett Anderson much because we had insurance. We could bill him for the deductible. The gas tank was also nearly empty, but he was buying that anyway. We stopped for three minutes at the hotel to pick up our suitcase and then headed for the tollway that led to Oaxaca.

San Cristobal de las Casas is a great town full of obvious charm, but I can't say any of us looked back other than to see whether we were being followed.

"How's the weather in San Miguel this time of year?" said Megan from the back seat in an artificially casual tone of voice.

"It's December there too, so don't bother to unpack that bikini," Maya said.

We were on the road again.

CHAPTER FIFTEEN
THE LONG ROAD HOME

Unfortunately there is only one sensible way to get to Oaxaca from San Cristobal, so we had no illusion that Nathan's crew wouldn't be able to guess where we were headed, should they decide to come after us. From the Guanajuato license plates they knew we were not going to be headed for Tabasco.

"This is the right thing to do," Megan said with a brighter note in her voice, as I blew through the streets at an indecent pace. "I guess I could've stayed in San Cris but they would've caught up with me there. I was just foolish enough to play the role of Martin Luther to Brother Nathan's pope."

"What will happen to your followers?" I said.

"They'll probably go back to Brother Nathan. The Catholic Church doesn't have much going on there anymore, and the Maya were never that loyal to it anyway. They preferred their own ways whenever they could get away with going back to them."

"How far will they travel?" said Cody. "The Nathanites, I mean."

"Well, they know where you're from and that it's halfway across the country. They might come up that far, or maybe they won't. But at least they don't know what city you live in. Guanajuato is a big state."

While the others were practically giving each other high fives over our improvement in security I was thinking about the fact that I had given our innkeeper my business card when we checked in at the hammock zone in Mazintla. It showed our address and phone number. Since our house key was on the chain of car keys they'd gotten at El Toro Verde, this was looking more like no security at all. I decided not to say anything to diminish the cheer, but the risk I'd created was not hard to assess and worth some further consideration during the trip. Changing the front door lock right away when we got home would be a priority.

It was dusk when we left San Cristobal, and after a long stressful day none of us wanted to go much farther; just enough to evade the Nathan group so we could get some sleep in an anonymous town and start fresh in the morning. On the map Cody found a place called San Mateo about 130 kilometers up the highway and we decided to stop there if it offered a reasonable place to stay. After our spare quarters in Mazintla, it wouldn't take much to look appealing.

Cody spent a few minutes working over the pistol we'd taken from one of the thugs at El Toro Verde. Finally he handed it to Megan. "Do you know how to use one of these?"

"My dad has one. It's bigger than that one, though."

"The principle is the same; keep the safety on until you plan to use it."

In the fading light the pine forest continued on both sides of the highway. Soon the sky was nearly black. I don't like to drive in México at night because of the hazard of roving animals, but in this densely overgrown area no cattle would be wandering free. Soon the altitude was dropping and the air felt warmer. We had of course lost the GPS with the sound system, but the route was familiar and well marked. There was no reason to think that the worst was not behind us. Even if Brother Nathan decided to pursue us, they would have to scramble to put together a vehicle on such short notice. Even with God on their side, they couldn't be *that* good.

Soon Maya and Megan were chatting about San Miguel and what life was like there. Had Megan made some conciliatory overture to her? That would be helpful. All of us were relaxing as the kilometers ticked off along the darkened highway, a genuine freshly paved route that seemed like part of the twenty-first century for a change, although modern times is not usually what

México does best. We saw little other traffic. I was trying to picture a quaint and charming hotel in old San Mateo. We could be having a nightcap and unwinding at the bar, maybe a Bacardi Añejo on the rocks. Cody was always partial to rum and we could sit around the table beneath something other than oil lamps and trade horror stories about Mazintla in tones softened with grateful relief. Maya would have a shooter or two of good tequila the way she did when she wanted to break an evil spell we'd fallen under. And I could see Mazintla as a cursed place myself, ground into fragments between the millstones of endless poverty and the mindless tyranny of Brother Nathan. It was too early for an end of case review, but certainly a breather was in order.

Megan, of course, would have lemonade made with mineral water. If San Mateo had any shops, in the morning we might be able to replace some of the clothes we'd lost in the suitcase we abandoned at El Toro Verde. Maybe Megan could find something else that would fit her current dimensions. Soon we'd be settling into a room with a bed that included a real mattress. We had once again become simple people with simple needs, and it felt good. Maybe the guns would come out again tomorrow, but for now, we seemed to be home free.

When we passed the first exit sign for San Mateo half an hour later there was an audible sigh. Three kilometers further on another sign told us that the

San Mateo exit was closed. No rationale was given, but we all knew the unspoken reason: this is México, where fate will sometimes take you by the throat when you least expect it.

"Shit," said Cody and Megan almost simultaneously. He shuffled in the glove box again for the maps.

"At least we're not looking for a place to eat," said Megan. "Although I should've gotten another one of the those cinnamon buns to go. You know, just for later in case breakfast is late in the morning. I also wouldn't mind peeing fairly soon."

I was starting to like our Scandinavian cult goddess more now, not that I'd ever disliked her. But meeting someone billed as a deity can make me kind of reserved for a while until I get better acquainted. Beyond the palm frond breastplates and the translucent skirt was a woman of unpretentious substance and fundamental needs. Like Cody, I had never been around any pregnant women for a prolonged period before, and her ordinary necessities and base-line focus were refreshing. If she had ever been frivolous, she had left that behind in Edina, Minnesota. I began to see her as more of an asset in her own rescue.

Cody mumbled for a while under the makeup light in the visor. "There's a place called Corral Hierba. It might be about another eighty kilometers or so. Can't tell from this map how big it is exactly."

"Is there an exit there?" said Maya.

"Don't know. This map is older than the tollway we're on. This route was only marked by dashes when it was printed."

Once I bought this Town and Country new with its GPS, I'd never updated the paper maps.

I didn't add anything to what the map offered. It could only be what it would be. Naturally we hadn't anticipated being on the run at night looking for a place to come to earth. By about 9:00 we had come fifty of those additional eighty kilometers when, cruising over a low rise, I spotted the red and blue lights of a police vehicle ahead. Apparently stopped on the shoulder, there was no way to tell why it was there. On these stretches of tollway the cars usually belonged to the *federales*. That was not alarming in itself, since they were rarely other than professional if you were not near the border, but it might indicate the presence of trouble ahead of another kind. Still, I didn't see any way it might connect to Brother Nathan.

"Any thoughts about this?" I said to Cody in a low tone.

"Drunk driving accident? I won't know till we get closer. This cop doesn't appear to be moving, so he must be signaling a problem ahead."

Across the highway from the first set of head-lights another cluster lit up. I slowed down a bit more. No other vehicles were moving on the tollway. I began scanning for any kind of exit in case it was a situation we felt compelled to avoid. We were still in Chiapas and it might be some outbreak of Zapatista unrest. Even though Subcomandante Marcos had announced his retirement, you could never know what might be on the minds of the rank and file, and their approach had a long history of hampering travelers to make their political points or pick up a little extra income. Maybe some candidate for his successor was flexing his muscles.

Barely a kilometer later we saw the roadblock. Well lit by search lights and eight or ten federal police vehicles with their headlights trained on them, a darkened tour bus was parked across the triple lanes on each side of the median. Nothing could move in either direction.

"This looks more like the *normalistas* than the Zapatistas," Cody said. These were the militant student teachers, whose far left views constantly put them in the spotlight as they disrupted every major highway they could. They had begun in and spread across Michoacán, then expanded their field down into nearby Oaxaca. In the horrible murder of "the 43" not too long ago, the 43 victims came from their ranks. Because of their ruthlessly disruptive behavior, including kidnapping, vehicle theft, and vandalism, they didn't always get the sympathy they deserved as murder victims themselves. Their most common practice was to steal buses, offload the passengers as hostages, and park them across highway lanes with flattened tires and the keys thrown away into the bush.

On the right my headlights picked up a dirt service road edging the pavement and I slowed down. A bit farther on, I began to see the taillights of cars drawn up on both sides of the highway. Beyond that point, halted cars clotted the entire pavement, stopped where they could go no further. I pulled off on the shoulder and backed up to the service road entrance. It probably went nowhere, but could we afford to be blocked and turned into an easy target because of someone else's militancy? Other cars would soon pile up behind us and block us in.

"At least this time it's not about us," said Megan thoughtfully. "But that's not much relief."

"Let's take a look at where this dirt road goes," said Maya wearily. "There might be a way around this mess."

She was not the only one whose patience was fraying. I pulled off onto the service road. Fortunately the sky was nearly as clear as in San Cristobal, so we had some intermittent moonlight to help us. The terrain was mixed trees and brush with some rocky outcroppings. It appeared to be drier here than in San Cristobal.

"We can't be that far away from the Oaxaca border," Cody said.

We were following a single-lane dirt road that

gave no indication of where it might be headed. Under my headlights the tire tracks were wide and ribbed with thick barred diagonal treads, like those on a large tractor. They were mixed with more conventional tracks. About a kilometer in I began to smell thick and greasy smoke on the air, but I couldn't see any flames ahead.

"What is that?" I said to Cody.

"Could be burning tires."

"I wonder if we're headed for the dump. Any thoughts?" I said into the back seat.

"It's better than being locked into a crowd of other cars on the highway," Maya said. Megan didn't offer anything.

After another half kilometer we went into a long shallow curve and came out on the edge of a gravel pit that looked about ten meters deep. I immediately cut the headlights when I saw the source of the light. A long ramp led from our road into the excavation, and beyond, near several tall mounds of loose gravel, we saw two more tour buses with their headlamps lit and next to them a huge bonfire spewing black, noxious smoke. At the edges intact tires were visible. The bus headlamps were aimed at a group of seventy or eighty people sitting on the ground clustered tightly together. About a dozen others walked about. Some carried rifles.

'Well," said Cody. "And what do we have here? Let's stash this van and check out the scene." His fingers automatically traced the position of the gun in his belt.

"Are you rethinking the highway now?" I said over my shoulder to Maya.

"No. Here we can still run into the hills if we have to."

I clung to the edge of the drop off until the road veered away and we ended up alone in a cleared and level parking area faced on three sides by rocky outcroppings. When we all got out into the chancy moonlight I locked the van. A cold wind swept in eddies across the barren landscape, dipping into the pocket where we stood. It was too dark there to make out the faces of the others. I wondered if we had reached a dead end, where the future depended on what the people around us were doing. Certainly we were greatly outnumbered; on the other hand, no one knew we were there.

Cody turned and silently marched off toward the pit, gun in hand. "Keep an eye on this end," he said.

CHAPTER SIXTEEN
CODY WILLIAMS

Cody slipped away from the others and in the darkness was soon nearly invisible. His principal question was whether anything was developing in the pit below, or was this merely another static standoff that could last for weeks? Often they were only about making headlines. With the Zacher Agency's risky mission they had no time to loiter in hopes of a settlement. He had never understood why the government was so slow to take action in cases like this, where dozens of people were being held captive and traffic on major thoroughfares was completely shut down. He had lived in México for eight years, but this reluctance to use some muscle to rescue people and clear the roads, or at least generate an effective settlement at the negotiating table was one of those things he still didn't understand.

The shock of the recent murder of 'the 43' in rural Ayotzinapa, in the coastal state of Guerrero. had caused a momentary lull in such acts of protest. Clearly they had now resumed, but what bothered Cody most was the thought that there might have been a precedent set by that unsolved crime. As he walked he scanned the obscure terrain.

From above the road they'd entered on, a sharp rise wandered off to the south. It started gradually and rose steadily for at least the next hundred meters, which was all he could make out. In charting its upper profile against the partially moonlit sky he could see that it must command the full range of the action in the gravel pit. He would've seen the same view by standing on the edge of the excavation, but then his profile would be exposed to the changing background light. Moving onto the shadowed slope he began to climb higher in cautious silence.

He had not gone forty meters when he noticed, crouched among the rocks not far below, a man dressed in black cradling a rifle in his hands. Cody had caught a flicker of moonlight off the brighter metal of the scope, but his eyes were well adjusted and he soon made out the man's form as well. Resting in a small level space, the sniper was intently scanning the crowd in the gravel pit, the rifle supported by a stone outcropping that mostly shielded his body from view from below.

Cody found himself immediately facing a dilemma. Was this man a *normalista* sentry, watching for an approach by the police, or was he planning another 43-style massacre? If that were the case, he was probably not working alone. In extreme silence Cody moved past, trying to discover another niche in the hillside for a second gunman, or even more.

And what was the morality in that situation? The kidnappers below must have abducted two busloads of people, and possibly four, if the passengers from the two buses on the highway were part of this group. In Illinois, where Cody had been a homicide detective, kidnapping was usually punishable by a sentence of thirty years. Did that make this man a vigilante?

Even if it did, for Cody the fundamental starting point was always the rule of law, anywhere. Vigilantes had no special rights of any kind when the police authority was still functioning. They were merely killers wearing masks of morality.

He had just turned away to face the farther reaches of the rugged hillside, still in search of that second gunman, when he caught the unguarded sound of rapid footsteps approaching on the gravelly path. The man below him heard them too, and shifted his gun toward the rocky approach Cody had used.

Cody whirled around. He was appalled to see the moonlight catch Megan's blond hairdo in the Mazintla style as she sprinted awkwardly up the slope, her arms extended for balance in the obscure light and uncertain footing. The man below him quickly raised his rifle and leveled it at her.

A natural reaction perhaps, but Cody wasn't taking any chances. In a single gesture he dropped the four feet to the man's side and threw his fist into his right ear. The man was lifted from the ground and landed on his side motionless. Cody seized the rifle, ejected the cartridge from the chamber, pulled out the clip and threw them both as far as he could into the brush covering the hillside. Swinging the rifle by the barrel, he smashed the trigger guard flat on the stone outcropping until the trigger was immovably locked in place. Then he dropped the gun next to the unconscious man. When he climbed back onto the upper path, Megan ran into his arms.

"I was so worried about you!"

Cody felt like slapping her for the danger she'd caused, even as it came to him at that moment that he couldn't solve any of this. The forces in play were too large and to get in further would only put the others at risk. The first priority was to get Megan out of there.

"You shouldn't have come out here," he whispered. He stopped himself from saying anything further.

They were still holding each other tightly as Paul and Maya ran up, no smarter, he thought, than Megan had been.

We're all too damn tired, he thought. Let's just get the hell out of here and find a way home before something else happens.

CHAPTER SEVENTEEN

I hadn't lived in México for long before I came up with a name for its distinctive domestic driving style, one I had seen nowhere else. I named it *freestyle driving*. It is at once loose and creative, open to the entire range between subtle whim and broad gesture. The sweeping and graceful moves remind me of Isadora Duncan in her prime. It admits of no road rage, since it is a joyous, uplifting display of virtuosity in which rules are not there to be broken—they are mostly not even there at all. It's like an interpretive dance, spiritual and nuanced, but executed on four wheels.

For someone like me, who uses painting as his main creative outlet, potential wildness is not the principal charm of driving as it can be for some others. I was ruined by driving in the States until I was twenty-three. For me, safety still counts, as does a minimal level of predictability in what's happening around me on the pavement.

Nonetheless, as I left the unpaved gravel pit road

and headed southeast back toward San Cristobal, we were going in the wrong direction on the divided high speed tollway because there was no way to cross the median. I knew that neither my motives, my sobriety, nor my sanity would be questioned by any other driver I might meet coming toward me in the dark. In the States, of course, where such behavior is a capital offense, I would've been instantly surrounded by a roving mobile swat team and gunned down before I could leave my driver's seat.

México has a lighter touch, and a more accommodating respect for individual tastes, even in driving. Beside me in front, Cody was not complaining about it, although I sensed in his attitude a residual discontent with our performance at the gravel pit, but Megan was making distressed noises in back.

For Maya it was nothing new at all. Growing up in Mexico City, where this kind of performance was long ago brought to a high art, she was a connoisseur of freestyle driving. And I might add, no mean master of it herself.

I won't say that returning this way was my first choice, but even if we had gotten across the median, we could still only go back in the direction we'd come from, if somewhat more conventionally. Of course, by that time none of us was very fresh. We had begun the day by leaving Mazintla at about seven in the morning. It was now nearly ten o'clock in the evening.

There was not much traffic on the highway at that hour and I made a point of flicking my headlights at each oncoming driver. If they didn't flick back, I pulled onto the shoulder while they passed. I will admit that as the kilometers rolled by, this retrograde journey took on an increasingly surreal quality. Not that Mazintla had ever looked like Main Street, USA.

"Where are we going?" asked Maya softly after a while, leaning forward as if afraid she'd awaken the others. Driving the wrong way on a super highway at night was no reason to stay awake. Cody lurched upright with a subtle grunt and fumbled for the map, pulling his reading glasses out of his pocket. He turned on the makeup light and his finger ran blindly down the page.

"It would be a place closer to San Cristobal that we rejected when we left as not being far enough away," I said. "Now it's going to look like home, whatever it might be."

"Then it could be San Andres," said Cody, looking at me over his glasses. "It's really too close to San Cristobal to be that comfortable, but it has the advantage of also being on a different normal highway that goes our way too, probably through the mountains. We'd be able to rejoin the tollway somewhere on the other side of the Oaxaca border. We could hole up there tonight and take that other route in the morning. I have no hope that the situation we just saw is going to break up soon.

Certainly not in time to meet our needs, anyway."

This received everyone's vote. In a situation with no good options, falling back on the democratic process often makes the most sense. It's a system that respects principle, and in using it you can blame everyone else when it fails and they'll all feel good about it, since they used the right process to make a bad choice. I knew Cody would respect this too since so much of his working life had been structured around procedure.

Anyway, that's what logic looked like that night as we courted a head on collision with anyone who had forgotten to turn on his headlights. If we were mentally frazzled, we were no less so physically. I was feeling vulnerable myself, as if in a crisis I wouldn't be able to respond very fast.

Twenty kilometers further on I pulled into a Pemex gas station from their exit lane. It being México, where this kind of independent-mindedness is, if not applauded, at least respected, no one seemed to notice it. We all ran for the restrooms while the attendant filled the tank. Megan was the last to rejoin us, laden with potato chips, four bottles of water, five candy bars and three bags of nuts of different kinds. Her arms might have held more, but this had exhausted the rest of her cash from Mazintla.

Cody was at the wheel as we pulled away from the gas station. Maya had moved up front with him and

I was seated behind him next to Megan.

"Tired?" I said softly to her, wanting to reach out to her more than that, but I knew Maya would be irritated. I understood how Cody was feeling about her, since Megan's condition and her flight from potential assassins made me also want to be her bodyguard.

"Exhausted." She pressed my hand and released it. "I'll be sleeping for two if we ever come to earth." She placed one hand on her abdomen. "This little person is wasted too."

As I looked back at her I suddenly saw her as part of the scriptural legend of King Herod plotting against her as the Madonna with her unborn baby. Usually I only do religious subjects as copies of much older Spanish colonial work, but I could easily paint Megan in that setting.

We were silent for a while, cruising along against the traffic, which was light enough that we encountered only one car about every kilometer or so. It was helpful that we hadn't met any police. They may all have been collected up at the roadblock. How little the rules matter, I thought. Necessity is the biggest rule now, perhaps the only one. Ragged as we all were, there wasn't much we wouldn't do to get home.

"I think I'll have to write about this," Megan said after a while. "Not anything scholarly, only a factual narrative of what happened, you know, and how it happened. It really went fast, once it got going. It was hard to think about because it changed every day, and it was nothing that Leo and I ever expected. Maybe now, I mean once we're settled somewhere, I could pull the story together to make more sense. That is, if we had a little peace and no more worries for a while."

My experience prompted me to keep my own counsel about that idea.

"It's not over," said Maya. "You said that yourself. We're still running and we don't know where they are."

"When I write it I won't put that part in, though. My story would be about the group dynamics, not like this."

"Small groups have dynamics too," said Cody without looking back at us. "We still have those dynamics right now, maybe more than we want."

"You're scaring me," I said with a smile only Megan could see.

Her statement about writing this story made me wonder how Megan viewed what had happened since the Zacher Agency appeared in Mazintla. "Is our arrival a break in the story, or one of its necessary elements?" I said.

"I think both. The end would've been different if you hadn't come, but the arc of the storyline was already fractured when you arrived."

"Wouldn't you have died too?"

"No. I think I would've ended up as Brother Nathan's slave. That would've been more satisfying to him. Or maybe he would've died in a struggle between the two sides, but I think I would've survived in that case."

"Why is that?" said Cody, still focused on the oncoming traffic, but with one ear following this.

"Nathan isn't spiritual in the way I am. He's a cynical pretender, kind of like all the politicians that get elected by promising to give things away. 'I'm offering you a seat at God's table,' he would often say, as if those seats were his to dispose of. That was his favorite line. 'How can you refuse it when so few are invited?'"

"I thought you said you weren't religious," said Maya.

"I'm not. Sometimes I think religion debases spirituality by using it for its own ends. I don't know. I'm probably not making much sense anymore." She rubbed her face with both hands. "I would so love a hot shower and some clean clothes that actually fit me. You know what? I'll say it. I'd really like to look attractive again to some good-looking guy, even just for a little while. I'd like my hair to straighten out and shine, and my skin to be clean. And I'd like to smell good and not be bulging out of my clothes. Even my bra doesn't fit anymore."

"How do you feel about Leo now?" I said, ready to move on from that image.

She responded with a long sigh. "You have to know that I've thought about that nonstop. I don't think I was ever in love with him, but when he just disappeared like that I realized what a good friend he was, and how much he supported me. Suddenly I felt like a table with only three legs. He wasn't great, but he wasn't a bad guy either. You hate to see someone like that taken out, because I never demanded that he be great, you know? I think I always knew his shortcomings. Anyway, he was like the rest of us. That's where I came to rest with it."

"Do you think Leo was in love with you?" Maya said, turning with her head between the front seats.

"He said he was, and maybe he meant it. I'll never know now. He was very eager in bed, but it isn't so much what you say to someone in a heated moment, it's what you go through together, day by day. That's what I took from his disappearance to bring to the people who came to hear me in church. Most of them had been through the loss of someone like that, so they could connect. Mazintla always had an air of tragedy about it, more than any other place I've been. That town was tired of life and looking for something else."

I wanted to ask her what she thought that was, but I saved that question for a time when we were all fresher. We drove on for a while, calmly in that insane flight from the blockade. Nothing made much sense anymore on the highway, and I thought Megan's summary was as good as anything.

"Could Nathan be another Jim Jones?" said Cody, moving on to a new subject that I knew was heavy on his mind now that we were on the road. He must have been trying to evaluate Jones's control of his followers in terms of what we might be facing at home. Could Nathan order someone to kill Megan without coming along himself?

"Never. If all his disciples died he wouldn't have anyone to order around, and he was too vain to kill himself. One reason I understood him so well was that I saw a bit of my dad in him. It was all about control, more than principle."

This prompted me to ask myself whether she had only fled one devil by running into the arms of another without realizing it.

"What was Nathan's appeal for Leo?" I said.

Megan didn't respond for a while. In the dim interior light her hands were fidgeting, her fingers wrestling with themselves. "He had read an online article about Nathan and he admired what he had done in building a new congregation just by the force of his will or personality, the way he'd reinvented himself as a spiritual leader. Leo didn't say this, but I always wondered whether he didn't want to imitate Nathan himself. Maybe Leo wasn't ready to admit that yet. There were times when my own church was starting up that I felt Leo looked at himself as the power behind the scenes, and I was like this figurehead, a tame saint he could send out to make the audience cheer."

"Isn't that like any church?" Maya said in a sympathetic voice. "The divinities are all made of painted wood and plaster, or bread and wine, but the priests have all the real power. They're always acting in the name of this or that saint or god."

"Probably. But when Nathan had Leo killed it took the process to a different level. I still don't understand what that meant for him. It's going to take me a while to figure it out."

"It was raw power," said Cody. "Changing life into death is no less powerful than changing death into life. Think of Lazarus. In either case it's the power of life and death."

"Killing is usually part of that process," I said. "Starting with Christ himself, the Romans killed a lot of early Christians in trying to stop the threat of that new cult. Once the Catholics came to power later they killed anyone who disagreed with them, often by burning them at the stake. When its time came, Islam spread across Africa and Asia at the point of a sword. And you know what's happening today. I think Nathan has gotten it right, within the tradition where he's operating. Spare no one that doesn't kneel down to you. Kill everybody else."

No one responded to this. The kilometers rolled on in silence for a while. I knew Maya was getting sick of religion talk. She hadn't added to this.

"I've been watching the rear view mirror for the exit signs," Cody said, "since they're only facing us once we go past. When we reach San Andres we'll be beyond the northbound exit by the time we know what it is, so we'll just swing around in a U-turn and come in like normal people from the inbound lane."

"It's great that they're all lit," I said. Coming back toward San Cristobal, exits had been rare, although I had seen a number of underpasses beneath us that offered no access from the tollway, merely routes for the locals to get from one side to the other.

Some time later we entered a stretch of the highway with extra lighting mounted on overhead signage for points beyond. We passed a ramp leaving in the direction we'd just come from, and then an unknown exit leading toward a town. If there was a sign on the ramp we couldn't see it. A hundred meters farther on the sign for San Andres appeared behind us. Cody swung over on the shoulder to wait for a pair of headlights to pass before we turned around.

As it came into view I had an eerie sensation. A number of vehicles had slowed to look at us in passing. Free style driving accommodates many varieties of expression, but going long distances the wrong way on the tollway clearly broke new ground for some witnesses. I was not normally a trendsetter in painting, and I wasn't enjoying it now in driving. The vehicle coming toward us, just passing under the overhead lights, was a battered red fifteen-year-old Chevrolet pickup; a crew cab model with oversize knobby tires. My visual memory is often close to exact, and I knew I had seen this truck on the high road to Mazintla as we went in. I had also painted a number of pictures using old wrecked vehicles, so the textures, wrinkles, and the color of rust were all familiar visual terrain for me. This was the truck we passed before we encountered the break in the road, the one where Artemio Díaz could've shaken hands with the driver without leaning out of his window. It might also have been the vehicle we had seen dropping Brother Nathan off at his new church, but I was less certain of that because of the darkness.

The truck slowed sharply as it passed us, and the driver's head spun around to look us over.

"It's them!" Maya practically squealed from the front seat.

Cody spun out and around in a rush. We had to get off the tollway fast—there was no room to maneuver there, no concealment or cover available, and this was no place for a shootout, even though I was certain we possessed more firepower than they possibly could. None of us thought there could be more than one reason for that truck to be there. We whirled in a half circle into the right lane toward the exit. Already past the ramp, the pickup wheeled around, nearly rising on two wheels. We pulled off without slowing. The van was not that fast, but it was faster than a relic of a Chevrolet pickup whose last tune up was probably an unfulfilled dream.

Of course they had only seen us before as we rode in the Land Rover, so either these were people who'd been furnished with a description of a white Town and Country with Guanajuato license plates, or they were the folks who had seen us drive past in our recovered van on Díaz' street as Cody gave them the princess wave with an offensive grin. From Megan's description one of them had to be Brother Nathan.

Now we were being summoned to appear for Judgment Day in Chiapas. Or Judgment Night, depending on who won this game of hide and seek.

"Lock and load," said Cody gravely as we streaked along the exit ramp into the darkness and the unknown. The town of San Andres was not sited directly on the tollway, so for a time we were passing through open country. I felt Megan's hand take mine as if she knew what was coming and she didn't care to face it alone.

CHAPTER EIGHTEEN

Although the exit ramp was recently paved, after a hundred meters or so it merged with an older two-lane highway with no shoulders that must still have passed beneath the path of the present tollway. It was not lit, and after crossing through two deep cuts in the terrain that were spread along a shallow curve, we came out onto a gently rolling landscape. Away from the tollway lights, the sky yielded a dim glow through thin streamers of clouds that was almost functional for driving blind in an emergency. Cody slowed slightly and switched off the headlights.

"Now I wish the van wasn't white," Maya said.

After about half a minute a pair of headlights appeared behind us on high beam, coming out of the curve. Cody sped up again. Any cow that wandered into our path would've ended up in our laps.

"Cody, can you still see?" said Megan. "How fast are you going?"

"I don't know. When the headlights are off the

speedometer isn't lit. I'm just goin' as fast as I can and still stay on the road."

The truth was I didn't know how good Cody's night vision still was. He sometimes wore reading glasses, and that could mean his long distance vision might be better, but you never knew. He was straddling the white line on the center of the pavement well enough. By craning my neck I could see the headlights behind us again. They didn't seem to be gaining or losing. The pavement was a little rough, but we hadn't hit any holes or speed bumps. If we suddenly entered San Andres this could turn into a Wild West shootout on Main Street.

"Would it make any sense to have the headlights on again?" said Maya. Her voice was elaborately casual, as if she'd been smoking grass as the police cruised slowly past.

"No. I'm going to get off if I see a good spot and I'm hoping they don't see me do it."

We went another couple of kilometers at about the same pace. As we moved into a long slow curve the moon appeared more clearly, lighting an offshoot road to the right. Unpaved, it went on for about twenty meters until it passed behind a rustic white blockhouse of some kind, with a flat roof and square perimeter and no visible windows. A clump of trees started up at the far back corner. Without a word Cody slid off too fast and skidded to a stop behind the blockhouse, just as I caught the glow of the headlamps coming into view behind us.

"I think your brake lights would've come on," I said.

"I was trying to time it until I got behind this building."

We all held our breath. From where we'd stopped we couldn't see the pickup pass until it was far beyond us. We waited. I heard the subtle sound of clothing shifting as all four guns came out.

"Keep those safeties on," said Cody, now the platoon sergeant. "We don't want to shoot ourselves up in close quarters." He opened his door soundlessly and got out, slipping behind the far corner of the building and peering through the thin line of trees facing the highway. Before he left he must have dialed the van lights down to nothing because they didn't come on when he opened the door.

The rumble and creak of an old pickup with loose parts became audible on the bumpy pavement. The sound grew closer, not slowing down or speeding up. The headlights came up, still on high beam, and then passed on the other side of the blockhouse. Beyond, the pickup's single flickering taillight moved away into the darkness a second later, disappearing for an instant behind each tree. When it was gone Cody climbed back in.

"Well done, big guy," said Megan. "We'll live to preach again."

"Thank you and amen, Sister Anderson."

"Now we wait until what? Does he turn around to see if we got behind him?" Sliding my pistol back in my belt, I rolled down my window to discover a subtle scent of smoke on the air. Of course, there was no shortage of firewood here.

"It's a country road near a town," said Maya, with a shrug I couldn't see but knew was there. "So it should lead into San Andres. Where else is there to go if you're pointed in that direction?"

I leaned forward and put my hand on her shoulder, feeling the weariness coming out of her. After another five minutes when nothing moved back on the main road, we started up again and followed our unpaved lane with our headlamps on, sheltered as we were within the random scatter of buildings. The borders of the road were occasionally fenced, with the small houses and cleared areas separated by dense stands of trees, almost as thick as jungle. Lights were rare. Next to me, a deep sigh came from Megan. She rested her folded hands on her abdomen.

"My hair is going to start to relax soon," she said. "It's going to look awful for a while. Just put up with me, OK?"

Fashion means safety, I thought. They go together. Going to a hairdresser to work on it would be a good bet on the future. At that moment we came to a T in the road. The sparse lights of San Andres glowed on the left about half a kilometer away.

Turning toward them, Cody kept within the darkened streets until we stopped near a small plaza. On one side sat a medium-sized church that reminded me of the one in Mazintla. A small hotel with an arcaded façade faced it across the open space. The other two sides had a series of one-story commercial buildings, with only one still lit, a cantina. The sound of jolly ranchero music leaked into the street from the louvered half-doors. One man sat on the curb outside holding his head with both hands, elbows on his knees, with his straw hat beside him on the stone pavement. No traffic was moving.

We pulled around the corner on the side of the hotel and unloaded our gear in darkness. I was on full alert, both ears up and listening as I set our suitcase on the pavement. Megan slid her backpack over her shoulders and we went in to find some rooms. Real beds, I thought, at last.

The hotel lobby was tiny, as if it had been a small front parlor in a home at one time. A sofa and two leather armchairs faced a mesquite coffee table with three or four newspapers fanned out on it. On the wall above, Emiliano Zapata glowered into the room from a framed sepia photograph, a small man with a lot of attitude. The furnishings looked ancient and worn, although quite clean. An older woman with her graying hair in a bun looked up sharply at us from behind a small desk, as if she'd nodded off. On a shield-shaped wooden board behind her were hooks for six keys. Five sets were present. Maya started to check us in with her credit card.

"While you do that I just want to give a note of thanks up at the church if it's still open," Megan said. "Can you get me a room next to yours?" This she addressed to Cody. He nodded and took her backpack.

"I'll go with her," I said. "This shouldn't take long." Maya always had final say on our room anyway. She said she would hide the van once she checked us in.

Even though Megan and I walked along the arcaded side of the plaza opposite the cantina I was still feeling too exposed. I kept my hand on my gun; I didn't know where her small revolver was. It seemed a little risky to have it tucked into her elastic waistband next to the baby. The clouds had moved in and nothing was lit in the sky anymore. She walked along in silence between me and the storefronts. Ahead, the church doors were closed but I could see light around the edges. When we reached the entrance the small door opened at my touch and we stepped inside. The time was about eleven o'clock, and the church was nearly empty but for eight or nine people close to the front. Candles and a pair of overhead lamps on cords hanging from the ceiling lit the altar, and wall sconces showed the way along both margins. We walked up a side aisle and paused at a display Megan selected.

In the candle rack before us only three votives were lit, short blunt candles in tapering glass containers. The smell of burnt wick and melting wax was thick on the air. The statue above, protected from dust within a dusty glass box, was one of Christ stumbling under the weight of the cross, slumped down onto one knee. He was wearing a belted white robe curiously unsoiled by the torture he'd endured. Although blood streamed down his face from the crown of thorns, none had reached his clothing.

There was only one part of the Catholic Stations of the Cross devotions, where this scene came from, that I found appealing, and that was where Veronica rushed forward from the other bystanders with a cloth to wipe the sweat and blood from Jesus' face. In the legend, it would have been just about at this point. Naturally, in the way of other religious moments, his image had remained on the fabric when she was finished. This cloth still exists, we are told, somewhere in Italy. Quite simply it is called *the Veronica*. Like that of the Holy Shroud of Jesus in Turin, I love stories like this because they are usually pious frauds, and art forgery is a subject that has long fascinated me. The challenge is always to figure out what the object *really* is, since artifacts of any kind inevitably have their own story to tell, no matter how their maker intended them to be understood.

With her eyes downcast, Megan appeared to be

meditating beside me, silent and absorbed in the scene. She had told us she had no religion, and she was not looking at the statue, but through the candles toward the floor. Her hands were clasped at the rim of the metal votive stand. A moment of silent prayer, I thought, spiritual but not religious, a distinction I had learned to make with her. I glanced around the church for an instant, not wanting to be blindsided, then turned back toward her. As if on casual impulse she reached out to the nearest unlit votive, and as her finger paused about two inches away, pointing at it with no particular force, the candle lit on its own. It simply came to life untouched by either of us. I remembered her comment during our first conversation about knowing a few spiritual parlor tricks, a remark I hadn't understood at the time.

Still, I blinked, telling myself I hadn't really seen this, since on looking back from the nave of the church, my eyes were focused slightly beyond the candle toward the Jesus box. I was still thinking of the Veronica, wishing I could touch that ancient scrap of fabric and hold it up to the light. I knew that even the weave would tell me something. But now what was Megan telling me?

"What was that? What did you just do?" I spoke rapidly, but quietly. Several other people were kneeling closer to the front of the church, but I didn't think anyone was near enough to hear me.

"You mean this?" She reached out and swept her

hand in an arc over the candle rack, and at least twenty others under the path of her index finger lit as well. I straightened up and took a sudden step backward.

"How did you do that?" It was a hiss, and my mouth must have stayed open.

She smiled, and leaning against me, spoke close to my ear. "It's only a parlor trick, Paul, nothing of any real significance. It comes from the energy in my fingers." She wrapped her right hand around my wrist, and the heat came off it into the flesh of my arm and hand. It was not searing, as if it was already cooling off. I jumped back and studied her face. Megan's clear blue eyes glowed in the half-light and her lips were slightly open. The flames of two dozen candles lit the edges of her front teeth. She still looked the same, a young pregnant woman without any makeup, one whose rumpled clothes needed washing, and whose hair required some attention. As close as we were to the hotel, she now had to be desperate for a shower.

I saw no supernatural gleam in her eyes, no vivid fervor. Our goddess on the run was as grubby and tired as the rest of us. "You have it too, you know," she said. "It's no big deal."

Palm downward, I held out my hand over the candle rack. Rather awkwardly, I discovered my fingers were shaking. Nothing happened. "I don't see it." Truthfully, I didn't want to see it. I didn't want to have to perform some cocktail party miracle at that point. I only wanted to go to bed.

"Maybe not now, but when you have a brush in your hand, that same intense energy is traveling down your arm and out into your fingers, and then through the handle of the brush to the tip. What comes out at the point where the paint meets the canvas is magical, but not miraculous. You must know that, since it happens every time you paint."

I thought her use of the worked *magical* overstated what happens. It would only seem that way to someone who didn't paint. Her feathery breath on my ear felt like it also possessed some vivid energy of its own, maybe from the same source. Involuntarily I put my hand to the side of my head and thought for a moment. At the sound of a cough from the front, I turned to see two women watching us from the second row.

"It's true that I can't articulate what happens at that instant of contact, brushstroke by brushstroke. But I don't need to and I don't try. Painting comes from the other side of the brain, the right side, where there is no speech. It has no words for things."

"Right, but you do know what I'm talking about now, don't you?"

I stared at my hand. "Did you use this power in your ceremonies?"

"Of course. It was part of the act. It gets people's attention, and it makes them think you possess some truth they lack. I really don't, but I may have access to some truths they also have but aren't aware of. Tell me you don't know that you can do things most other people can't. I know you do." Her whisper had grown more intense as she said this.

I looked into her face for a long moment, feeling that I knew less about her at that point in time than when we'd entered the church ten minutes earlier. Maybe I was only less certain about what I thought I had known. "No, you're right, Megan. But now I have another idea. You say this is no more than a parlor trick, a sleight of hand kind of event. Now tell me the rest of the story—what else can you do? Because I'm sure there must be more to this."

"You have some power too, I see. Call it insight." She turned away as a draft from the door opening at the front of the church caused a ripple to take flight through the lighted votive candles. At the side of her head I could see how the tightness of the curls was starting to soften and separate.

"Can you see me now?" she said softly.

"Better than you imagine. That's what I do. I could turn around and paint you with my back to you."

"That's because you're so close to me at this moment." She looked into my eyes.

"I can see the network of your irises in the candlelight," I said.

"But if you were farther away, I could make you not see me at all."

At first I didn't know whether to believe this, and I chuckled quietly, but uneasily. Sight is my home turf. No one can challenge me there and win. Many times I've kept painting a portrait when the subject walked away for a twenty-minute break. "Show me then, Señorita Bruja," I whispered, folding my arms.

"Turn and walk up toward the front. Go as fast as you want. When you get to the fourth row, turn around. I won't leave the building."

Thinking to give her plenty of time, I walked slowly to the front with an ironic grin, shaking my head. Three people sat in the fourth row, and the young man nearest the aisle looked at me curiously when I stopped and turned around, resting my hand on the end of their pew. He stuck his head out and looked down the aisle to see what I was staring at, but it was nothing. Megan Anderson was already gone.

This didn't surprise me. I knew she would've tried something. She'll be awkwardly lying on one of those narrow cushioned kneelers at the back of a pew, I thought. But this is a childish game. I decided to simply walk down the aisle to the main entrance.

However, by the time I reached the fifth row from the vestibule I had not seen her on either side. At a single step further I found her standing next to me, inches away. Her breath was warm on my neck. She had not materialized as if from some otherworldly cloud. Megan was solid and real, and she was simply standing next to me with no apparent motion required to get her there. The strings she was pulling were all in my head, gathered, it seemed, into a smallish knot she held between two fingers like the strings of a puppet. I suddenly recalled the comment of Ian, the man we'd met in the coffee shop on our first morning in San Cristobal. There was talk of a *bruja* heading a new cult in Mazintla, he'd told us.

"Go ahead and pinch me," she said, with what I thought was a rather salacious tone for a pregnant goddess.

"You're damn good, Megan. And I just realized something else. Now I know why that red pickup went past on the exit without stopping to look for us on that offshoot. He couldn't have seen us, could he? Even if our brake lights went on as we pulled behind that blockhouse before he was past. You did that to him, too."

Megan nodded slowly. "Yes. They were just far enough away for it to work. I wasn't sure it would."

"What else can you do?"

She shook her head. "Nothing much. It's all sophomore level goddess tricks. I couldn't raise anyone from the dead, for example, even Cody, if it came to that."

"Too bad. I hope it doesn't."

"I know. Me too."

I heard the buzz of hoarse whispering now coming from the front pews. "But what makes it happen?" I looked at her candidly.

She shrugged. "It's only will power. Don't you find you can make things occur just because you want them to? You can insist that they happen, and if your desire is great enough, then they do? Maybe for you that only occurs when you're painting, or investigating a case."

I could see this argument, although it never seemed extraordinary to me. "Yes, but none of those things falls outside the laws of nature. It's not like what you're doing."

Her eyebrows went up. "Why do you think this does? How often do you look at a scene and miss many parts of what's there? That's why eyewitnesses are so unreliable. They're not trying to see everything, so they miss a lot without realizing it."

"So you weren't blocking me from seeing you."

"No. You must have been looking at something else. What was it?"

"I was looking at the kneelers behind each pew, thinking that's where you'd be hiding."

"There you are. You weren't looking at me, so you didn't see me. In my own mind I nudged you toward looking at the kneelers. Maybe I planted that idea, but that's not magic, Paul. I don't know any magic. I'm just a recent anthropology graduate who's looking for a job."

I was frowning, unable to probe further into this, to get behind the parallels she was drawing. "When did you discover you could do things like this?"

"It was about a week after we arrived in Mazintla, and at first I just kept quiet about it. It's really no big deal. Usually I don't even want to discuss it, unless it's someone I really trust. And I have to trust you."

"Do you think that ability was somehow connected to being in that place?"

"Do you mean there are vortexes or emanations of some kind there? Is it like Glastonbury or Stonehenge?"

"Yes, I suppose."

She looked at me as if I was looking for something that had never been there. "It's only a dump, Paul, and a very sad one. That's what I thought when I got there with Leo, and that's what I thought the day I left. The only redeeming feature Mazintla had was the people that lived there."

"So these spiritual parlor tricks are all about you, and nothing else, not the place, not the occasion. And certainly not about religion."

"I'm not always sure I know what religion is."

I stood there for a moment thinking about her response. Leo had found something he thought of as spiritual in Megan, some undefined power. More than half the congregation of Brother Nathan had split off to join her reluctant ministry. I was left with the old sensation that comes over me so often in México of not knowing what I was looking at.

Initially I had felt a bit standoffish about her. I was uneasy about a trust fund kid from a privileged background in Edina who'd walked in off the street and been promoted to a novice goddess. The way I'm wired I rarely warm to pundits or gurus. I've spent a lot of time searching in my life, but I prefer to do it by following my own path with no one offering me pointers down this or that fork in the road. Maybe that's naïve, but it's taken me a long way in painting. I was still searching Megan's face for more answers when I also realized I was increasingly drawn to her in a way I didn't understand. She did have something I couldn't give a name to. I wanted to take her by the shoulders and pull her toward me.

"How long was it before Leo knew about what you'd discovered?"

"Not right away. It might have been three or four days after it started that he noticed it."

"What did he think?"

"He said it confirmed what he'd said about my spiritual qualities. But I didn't believe that. I told him some of what I just told you and he rejected it."

From the corner of my eye I could see a few people closer to the front were watching us, some still whispering. I took her elbow and guided her to the door.

"Will they come back?" I said. "The guys in the red pickup?"

"I don't know that any more than you do. Probably they will, if they realize we're not ahead of them on that small highway out of here. Or, they might go all the way up to San Miguel and wait for us. Or they might be somewhere between. The future is never visible to me. But I think we need to clean up and get some rest before we move on. We all need it. Then we'd be sharper for what's coming at us tomorrow."

We walked arm in arm back to the hotel. Again I was between her and the street and no one was under the arcades with us. When her hand casually touched mine I wondered if her skin was giving off a small charge. As I looked out around the plaza for anyone lurking, I could see that San Andres might almost be a charming town in daylight. Not that we would hang around in the morning. It would have to be in a time when we weren't fleeing across the country.

"What would you have done if I hadn't come away with you?" She made it sound as if we had run off together. Megan had that almost Mexican quality of displaying her awareness of your being male without mentioning it directly, that ever present male female polarity, as someone once called it.

"We had no real plan. We'd talked earlier about kidnapping you, but it didn't seem right."

"Then you would've had the whole troop after you, instead of only Nathan's death squad."

"I'm sure."

"I have a question for you," she said after a moment, "but you don't have to answer it."

"OK. Maybe I won't."

"Have you ever killed anyone?"

I sighed without meaning to. It's not a subject I enjoy discussing. With her I almost felt it was a confession. Maybe she could absolve me, since absolution is an outcome I still search for without success at times in my dreams. I wondered if Cody had mentioned something to her that prompted this question. "Yes. Several years ago I killed a federal police officer named Tomas León. I shot him in the back in a car as he was holding a gun to Maya's head."

A long silence followed and her arm tightened on mine. "Was that hard?"

"Only afterward. It's harder now. But you can't be successful in this business without being able to do that when the situation demands it. Is this a qualifications test?"

"I guess it is. I feel like I'm heading into something bad like that myself. I can't tell you why."

I stopped and faced her. "Megan, the Zacher

Agency was heading into something bad the day we left San Miguel. The day we met with your parents, in fact. You were up to your eyebrows in something bad in Mazintla. Having bad things happen around them is what makes people hire us. You can't sentimentalize this kind of work by saying you're helping people, because that's secondary. We're getting in the faces of nasty people and drawing a line in the sand in front of them, daring them to cross it. That's the only real way to look at it. You have to be ready to act bigger and meaner than they are, even when you don't always feel that way."

She nodded without comment and we walked on for a while. When the cantina music drifted across the plaza toward us we paused to watch. Two men now sat on the curb. One hugged the other in commiseration. A liter bottle of beer sat in the street next to his feet.

"Cody told me that Maya left the Agency for a while because she couldn't stomach the risk. He said she was tired of wearing a target all the time."

We started to move along again. Megan was looking at the uneven sidewalk lit by the meager lights in the shop windows along the loggia.

"That's right. She hated it. We had to make her head of the Agency to get her to come back."

"To get her to come back to you, was the way he put it." Surprised that Cody was so comfortable talking about Agency business with her, I didn't turn to look at her face as she said this, perhaps because I didn't want her reading mine.

"That's right too, because I wasn't going to shut down the Agency. We just needed to find a way to make it work better for her."

"But it seems like you still call the shots a lot of the time."

"Yes, but she picks the cases and makes other policy decisions. That's the key element for her in trying to limit risk. She also pays the bills and keeps the books and collects the money, but that first part was what she wanted most. Cody and I still do most of the day to day tactical stuff in the field."

"But that doesn't always work in limiting risk."

"No. For example, she thought this would be a simple missing person case, and that's what we all hoped."

She shook her head. "Nothing is simple. I've learned that much. All I wanted was to do some good and now people are trying to kill me." She paused for a while. "I suppose that's what your life in the Agency is like too, isn't it?"

"Most often that's true." We stopped in front of a shoe store window near the end of the block. Megan leaned against the stone sill with her hands gripping it on both sides. Behind her a display of Crocs in gumdrop colors glowed with faint luminosity in the low light. Under the arches, we could not have been very visible from the plaza. I looked into her eyes, feeling a kind of magnetism coming off her again. She stood up without warning and wrapped her arms around me, pulling me close to her. Her body felt solid and essential against me. I realized how much I had wanted to do this too. That close she smelled of the long drawn out day of worry and travel. She was weary and frankly a little dirty from the long motorcycle trip. I'm sure she had started the morning without much sleep, worrying about the people she was going to leave behind. As we all were, she was stretched to her limit, and there was nothing left alluring about Megan Anderson beyond her simple humanity, but that was enough.

"Thank you for this, Paul," she said, and kissed my cheek for a lingering moment. Then we walked across to the hotel, our heels resounding on the cobblestones in the empty night.

CHAPTER NINETEEN

Maya and Cody were waiting in the hotel lobby, silent, weary, and looking bored with two empty tequila shooters on the coffee table in front of them. It was a measure of how tired they were that they weren't finding anything to talk about. The desk clerk was nowhere to be seen.

"I thought you'd both be taking a shower," I said.

"We wanted to see that you got back OK. Anything happening out there? I looked out on the plaza a couple of times." The chair creaked as he leaned back.

"Nothing. Hardly anything is moving except for a few revelers at that cantina down the block." I sat down next to Maya on the sofa. She was looking back and forth between Megan and me as if she was picking up something lingering in the air.

"I don't think we need to have a sentry staying up tonight," she said. "The room doors bolt on the inside and unless a bullet comes through when you're standing there, I don't see much risk. The windows are barred."

Megan and I nodded. Cody and I could go to bed like normal people, but with our guns ready on the nightstands. I didn't want to think about having to function tomorrow with four hours of sentry duty and only three hours of sleep. Everyone wanted to go to bed and the conversation lagged again.

Upstairs, Megan had the room between Cody's and ours. We waited in the hallway until she was locked inside.

Maya showered first, without washing her hair, since the room didn't have a dryer and she had lost hers. When I came out after my shower she was wearing her pale blue cotton nightshirt that came to mid thigh, tucked in under the sheet and a single thin wool blanket. I walked around the end of the bed and hung my clothes on the back of the chair at the tiny writing table. Maya's were folded on the seat. The room was not large and it offered no wardrobe or closet. With dark red walls and a beamed ceiling, a single large window overlooked the side street where the van had first been parked. It was not there anymore, nor did I see anyone moving about.

"Well," she said as I climbed in beside her. "Are you Megan's newest best friend now?"

"Nope, just her bodyguard. Nothing new there."

"She didn't have to hold your hand in church? Maybe she was feeling faint from that aura of sanctity. It was familiar ground."

"Not that much."

"No other tricks?"

"Ah, yes, in a sense, one or two."

"Go on."

I told her about lighting the candles. Her eyes grew larger.

"Are you serious? Then she did put a spell on you." She sat up and tied her hair loosely toward the bottom with a violet ribbon, studying my face the entire time.

"Nothing I couldn't handle."

"What else?"

"She made me unable to see her."

"That must have been difficult with all the time you've spent looking at her."

"It didn't seem to make her short of breath at all."

"Did you tell her your visual memory is nearly perfect, right down to all the tiny little blond hairs on her upper lip?"

"I forgot to bring that up." I reached over and turned out the light, hoping that would shorten this interrogation. "Look, we're all worn out now. There's nothing happening between Megan and me. Let's be kind to each other and get some sleep." I kissed her goodnight.

In the morning the lobby offered us coffee and

a selection of fruit and pastries. None of us wanted to linger, and that was enough to get us launched on the road. I was startled to see Megan come down wearing a light green muumuu that looked fresh and clean, if a bit creased and wrinkled. It was not what a pregnant woman would ever wear here. Maya would've said muumuus are for overweight people. I'm sure she was thinking that, but she made no comment.

"I was going to save this for a special occasion, but I couldn't stand that skirt any longer. This really isn't my style, but a woman in my church gave it to me, knowing I'd reach this point. It is comfortable."

"The color isn't bad," I said, scraping for something positive to say about it. "There's enough blue in that green to play against your skin tones and hair." I could see painting her with some hint of those colors in the scene, but not the shape of that dress.

When we finished, Maya left to retrieve the van. No one else knew where it was. She was shaking her head as she went around the corner and walked past the window. The clarity and brilliance of the day made me feel optimistic. It promised a change we were all ready for. Our road into Oaxaca was going to be the old route. It would pass through the mountains and wouldn't always be maintained in the best condition anymore. At least most of the Oaxaca-bound traffic was now diverted onto the tollway, even though it was probably still blocked.

Not many would know that until they got there.

Still slightly paranoid, we were waiting in the shadow of the arches at the front of the hotel when Maya pulled up. Cody had Megan's backpack and I towed our suitcase around to the tailgate.

While Megan cautiously stayed back under the arches, in the blazing sun I surveyed the plaza with my hand shielding my eyes. At the corner on the left three people stood talking, a young man and two older women who did not have the Mazintla hairdo. No threat there, I thought. Closer to the church half a dozen people were going inside. Others were approaching. A few were just chatting on the steps. It looked like a normal morning in San Andres. No red pickups were in sight. I stepped into the street and lifted the tailgate. Maya got out and came around to the back, handing me the keys.

While I pushed the suitcase into one corner inside, Megan stepped forward from the shadows as Cody put in the backpack. The young man at the corner of the plaza quickly crossed the street and stopped about five feet in front of her. She looked at him in surprise. Cody put his hand lightly on her shoulder with a possessive and protective grip. I recognized the kid as the one at the end of the pew the night before where I had turned to find Megan had disappeared from the center aisle. I didn't think she would've recognized him now.

With the fingers of his right hand spread, he

reached out in her direction but didn't move any closer. "I would like to touch her garment," he said politely, apparently regarding the rest of us as her entourage. "I saw what she did with the candles last night. It was a miracle. We are so happy to have a saint among us." He crossed himself. Apparently believing this opening was going well, the two women now moved to join him from across the intersection. One had her hands reverently folded. Cody stepped briskly between the boy and Megan, as she cradled her swollen abdomen with both hands.

"What are you talking about?" he said gruffly. "She is not available for touching or anything else. We are leaving now. Please step out of the way. We'll be backing up."

"What happened last night is better forgotten," Maya said, mainly to the women, with an encouraging but tight-lipped smile.

"It was nothing," Megan said from behind Cody, not sounding well rested. It was a thinner voice than I'd heard from her before. "It was not a miracle. It was only a trick of the eye that had no importance, no meaning for anyone."

The older of the two women stepped forward. She wore a battered brown *rebozo* wrapped around her shoulders against the cool morning air. "But I saw it too. It was not a trick. She had no lighter or matches in her hand. First one lit by its own and then many more, all at once. Those candles are all gone now. People took them away last night to pray with on their home altars. The ones who got them are feeling blessed."

"We would like to be blessed too," said the other woman. She opened her hand to display a fresh votive candle.

The way Cody's eyes were shifting around among all of us suggested he had no idea what they were talking about. Megan and I had said nothing about the church when we came back to the hotel lobby. His right hand lingered near the hem of his shirt where the thin cloth covered his gun. Maya was starting to look irritated and reluctant to get any further involved.

"Please," I said, mainly to the women. "You will remember that I was in the church too last night. There was no event of any importance. Perhaps the breeze from the front doors blew the flame from one candle to the other. Standing so close to it, that is what I thought happened. This woman is just an American traveling here. She is not even of your religion and she needs to go home to have her baby now. We are leaving your pleasant town with good memories. I know that San Andres is a place that respects hospitality. As your guests, we also know when it's time to leave."

Had I possessed a pocket mirror I could've checked to see how long my nose had grown after that unbroken chain of whoppers. As I was speaking, four more people assembled across the street and started moving our way with no special urgency. Even so I felt the uneasiness among the four of us ratcheting upward by degrees, since the odds had shifted and we were now outnumbered.

"I don't care for the geometry of this," I heard Cody mutter between his barely opened lips.

"Please show the same respect for this woman's condition that you would to anyone among you," Maya took a step forward and said this in a voice of authority. Her accent had subtly changed into pure upper middle class Mexico City frosted with a growing note of impatience. "Nothing has happened here to merit your interest. Her husband is an important man in the federal police who is easily offended by bad manners (*mal educado* is how she said this). He will be arriving here shortly with his armed bodyguards to leave with her."

The crowd would now be picturing him stepping down from his polished black Suburban with smoked glass, surrounded by big anonymous men wearing sunglasses.

The women were now eyeing Maya coldly. The other four had already merged with the group. Several were whispering among themselves behind their hands.

"I only want to touch the holy woman's sleeve," said the single man among the latest four, removing his straw hat and holding it in his fingers. "I was told it is her right hand that made the miracle. I would like to kiss it."

"Yes! We would too!" echoed three or four of the women, even as one of the others was muttering sourly.

"You cannot stop us," another woman said. "This is church business. Please step aside now. We have important things to talk about with her. You are interfering with God's will. He will punish you."

I glanced back at Megan, who looked embarrassed, shrinking behind us with folded arms, staring off to the side, toward the shoe store where she and I had paused the night before. Her hands were tightly clenched in her armpits. The muumuu with the odd hairdo made her look both prim and ridiculous at the same time.

"Move back, all of you," said Cody in his big urban cop crowd buster voice. "We are leaving now. We don't wish anyone to be hurt as we pull out."

The young man from the church pew thrust his shoulders forward. "I think it is better that she stay here with us. There is a need for her in San Andres. We have some sick people here. Let her say what she wants to do, she can speak for herself. As a virtuous woman, we believe she will want to use her power to help us."

I had to admire the nerve of this kid, even though I felt like punching him hard in the face. Possibly he was a future mayor in the making. People would later recall how he had stood up to the arrogant gringos who were traveling with a saint and refusing to share her with people who needed her more.

Even though the morning was still young, the sun had somehow grown much hotter since this confrontation started, and I could feel the sweat trickling down my neck. No one in the crowd seemed to feel it. Cody stepped forward into the kid's face, hands on his hips. One was clearly touching his pistol, the lethal profile unmistakable beneath the hem of his oversize shirt. Maya and I linked arms and extended our other elbows to close ranks in front of Megan.

"You have no say in this," Cody barked. "She has told me what she wants to do, and I will see that she gets to do it because I am her father. Who intends to argue with me about this kind of private family business?" His big hostile face probed the crowd one by one as his finger pointed at each person. "Would it be you? Or you? Step out here in the open and talk to me if you think you can."

An ugly silence reigned for a long moment as five more people from the plaza joined the others. At the steps of the church beyond, more had paused and were looking back our way, shading their eyes. A few were pointing. The tension had become thick and palpable. My eyes searched one face after another, trying to get a sense of what was coming next.

Suddenly from the back edge of the crowd an arm without a face came up and launched a fist-sized rock at Cody's head. He ducked, but not quickly enough, and it grazed his ear before bouncing off the back bumper of the van.

He hurled the pushy kid back into the group, where, with a groan, he was caught by many hands. Cody pulled out his gun. Maya and I did too. They were all pointed skyward. A murmur of shock followed. Quickly it fell away into a hush. We faced more than a dozen wary looks but no one moved back an inch.

The extended lull that followed vibrated with unease. It was clear to me that we couldn't handle them all if they rushed us. My mouth was so dry I could almost feel grit between my teeth. I again looked from face to troubled face. The man in the back spat on the pavement. Here we were barely twenty-four hours out of Mazintla and we'd been forced into another religious crisis. I began to see Megan's spiritual qualities as more a curse than a blessing. Even though I still didn't understand them, I knew she was far too dismissive in calling them parlor tricks. From the corner of my eye I saw an increasing gathering standing just inside the other near corner of the plaza watching this confrontation. A few started to move our way from behind us. I felt like we were being outflanked. With no warning the front door of the hotel slammed shut out of sight on the other side of the van. A bolt was thrown with the startling impact of steel on steel. That was the only sound as we waited as if on a scaffold.

"Get in the van now, Megan," Cody said softly over his shoulder in English. "Keep your gun ready in your hand as you go in."

Many eyes followed her as, looking at no one else, she entered by the door behind the front passenger's seat. Maya turned and firmly closed the tailgate as if to put a period to this confrontation.

"I will repeat my question. Who intends to argue with me? Do you?" Cody thrust his rigid index finger into the kid's face an inch from his nose. Eyes downcast, he looked away.

Silence followed. The boy began vigorously rubbing his left shoulder as if he had only now realized that someone had grabbed him too hard to prevent a fall when Cody threw him backward. Everyone still wore a sullen look. With Megan behind the darkened glass in the van the crowd seemed to waver and lose some of its focus. Was the pressure starting to diminish? While they didn't try to stare Cody down, neither did they seem to know who else to look at or what to do next.

"It is time for all of you to go home now," he said in a less aggressive tone. "Nothing more will happen here today. My daughter has gotten into the van and she is going home too. She lives a long way away from here and she is not a saint. I can tell you that in all honesty. We are all sorry for this disturbance, which we did not intend to happen. Nor was it fate that caused it. It was a simple misunderstanding among people of good will on both sides. It is easily repaired if we all disperse now." His wary eyes moved rapidly over the crowd. They were mostly looking at his gun.

Locked rigidly on the sharp edge of this moment, no one stepped toward us or away, and the hostile stares still wavered. People shifted from one foot to the other as if rudderless. Seeming to search for a leader, a woman in front looked behind her. Even in that vibrating tension, I was struck by how normal everyone looked. These were identical with the people we said *buenos días* to every day on the streets of San Miguel.

From somewhere out of view a golf ball sized stone glanced off the top of the van and skittered into the loggia facing the hotel. Then one more, larger, was followed by a bounce and the delicately violent tinkle of shattered glass within the arches. Setting the tone for what was coming, the sound hovered on the air like a summons.

Taking their cue from this, another group of eight or nine people detached themselves from the concerned watchers in the plaza. They moved toward us in no hurry, as if we were already nailed down. One stooped to pick up something when he stepped off the curb, and suddenly the air crackled with increased anxiety. An unwelcome ringing arose in my ears like an alarm. The situation had reached a breaking point.

Cody lunged into the front edge of the crowd. Thrusting his gun closely among the heads of the four nearest people, he fired a deafening round straight up into the air. With screams of panic, covering their ears, they all fell back in confusion.

As we started to run for the van, two of them tumbled to the cobblestones as they fell back toward the plaza, screeching as they were stomped on by a dozen others. We didn't look back to watch them anymore while they began to scatter further away toward the church. We leapt inside the van.

The tires squealed as I floored the gas pedal. In a spatter of dust and gravel we spun away down a side street next to the hotel. Half of a brick sailed over the van and skipped down the pockmarked surface ahead of us. Then two more fist-sized rocks. Finally we heard only the sound of the engine revving and the tires hammering the ruts and rubble of the unkempt street. I didn't look back at the crowd writhing in the mirror. I knew what I would see there, and I had already seen more than enough.

CHAPTER TWENTY

Long ago we learned in the Agency that at a certain point in most cases the mind seeks order and calm. A place where you could stand with both arms outstretched and steady yourself between two nearby buildings as you catch your breath. At about one o'clock that afternoon, well beyond the Chiapas border into the state of Oaxaca, we stopped at a country roadside stand to buy bottled water and fruit, sausage and cheese, and four of those fresh bird rolls called *bolillos*; the makings for lunch. Resting in the locked van between two green fields in a broad level valley where we could see in all directions, the four of us ate in near silence. The lush indigo and violet mountains loomed around us. The sun had swept the filmy clouds away. We all felt bruised, and we were happy to be alone with ourselves.

Following our precipitous exit from San Andres, we hadn't talked much after Megan told Cody a diluted version of the church miracles that had gotten people so excited. It suggested that what she had done might have almost been an accident. Listening to it, the word *pyrokinetic* came to mind, a fire starter, but I didn't say it. If I didn't exactly agree with her spin on it, I added nothing. I couldn't read Cody's reaction, since his face was scanning a different part of the route than I was, but her story may have been so vague that he didn't appreciate its full significance. Or maybe I overestimated its importance. He surely didn't understand the reasons for its impact on the local people. Still, if only from the way she toned it down, it was clear to me that she deeply regretted her candle performance. It had looked to me at the time as if she was only showing off, even if I didn't understand how. Perhaps it was because she sensed her goddess status waning the farther we got from Mazintla and she felt it needed shoring up a bit. Without it, as she had suggested, she was only a recent college graduate looking for a job.

"I suppose it's a bit like those people who can walk on hot coals," he said. "I know that happens just from hearing about it from so many different people."

None of us had ever faced down a mob like that before, and the near miss aspect of it was too sobering to allow us to think of anything else for a while after we left San Andres. I'm sure they were all reasonable, honest people who had never previously done anything of that kind in their lives. That was the truly frightening part. While it was religion that had converted them into rock-throwing zealots, that confrontation also illustrated how ready they were to try to grab at something inspiring in their lives even if it was still out of reach. People in groups can do things they would never do on their own; the herd instinct seems to blunt their sense of individual responsibility. I glanced back at Megan, but her humbled features didn't respond. Hers was still a dangerous gift, even if she usually preferred to understate its importance.

I'm not much of a New Age person, and while I recognize that some people can do things that appear paranormal, I don't have any of those skills myself. While the explanation she gave me in the church made sense on the face of it, I still couldn't have done what she did. I know she would've responded that she couldn't do what I did with a paintbrush. But if she was so much more in command of herself and her abilities than I was of mine, how did she get into these scrapes so casually? Prudence is a spiritual gift too, not a parlor trick.

I could now see better how she had carved off more than half of Brother Nathan's following as if she hadn't really meant to. If, as she said, she hadn't developed a new theology in Mazintla, then she didn't need any. I don't know what Nathan was offering beyond certainty and crude authority, but his group was clearly susceptible to her more humanistic pitch. The San Andres crowd suggested how much desperation was out there waiting to be tapped into by the easiest of overtures, even the unintentional, or in Nathan's case, the highly cynical. Had killing Leo Cochrane mainly been Nathan's way of warning Megan to reel herself in a bit in his territory? He may have felt that killing her might have been too risky, and that Leo was a suitable surrogate.

While I still didn't think I knew her that well, I felt she was also something of a tease. Her church outfit had initially suggested that. Maya's antenna was certainly up in her presence, and that was the most reliable indicator I knew of. Sometimes a crisis like we'd had in San Andres will make people more transparent, will bring qualities to the surface that you might not ordinarily see, but Megan hadn't stood out in that crowd scene, other than as a target.

Even so there was clearly something about her presence that was, if not compelling, at least enticing. In her current somewhat dilapidated condition it was still a prominent part of her. I wondered about Leo Cochrane making love to her. Did he have any idea who Megan really was? Or did I? I made a mental note to have a private talk with Cody. He could bring his old psychology skills to bear here, unless she'd bewitched him too, which, from what I'd seen, was entirely possible.

As Megan blandly munched on an apple that early afternoon, her cheeks bulging slightly, a tiny trickle of clear juice ran down her chin. Sitting in the growing heat with the blousy skirt of her green dress tucked between her bare legs, I could also see her as a solid Midwestern farm girl. Perhaps Iowa more than Minnesota. Even so, I also began to wonder if she weren't more dangerous than I'd ever thought. Her version of what she'd done in the church bore no relationship to the influence it had on the local people who witnessed it. To me, that unintended effect was the essential reality of it, not what she thought she was so blandly doing with her open palm passing over a bank of candles. Was she like those women who casually get men to fall in love with them and then simply walk away as if they had no responsibility for it? I had known a few of those. I thought of them as hateful beauties, two words ill suited to be linked in the same sentence.

Although our task was to protect Megan, I was starting to wonder who was going to protect us from her casual recruitment of new fans. Cody could do confrontation better than Maya or me, but that still had its limits. We could've emptied all four pistols into that crowd and still been torn apart when the ammunition ran out. The timeliness of Cody firing his gun into the air at that precise moment had meant everything, and he fully recognized that the crowd scene had reached a tipping point. A larger gathering wouldn't have been dispersed so easily. The instant shock wave had given us just enough time to leap into the van and leave. Two minutes later would've been too late, since more people were advancing toward us from the plaza and the church steps.

Five minutes after the bricks and stones stopped flying we had left the scattered margins of San Andres and pulled back on the old two-lane highway going north in a better frame of mind. It looked like a day and a half to get home. Long enough, but I felt the worst was behind us. Somewhere out there was the crew in the red pickup, but their task was far larger than ours. They had to find us, while we only had to avoid them. Our odds were better.

"I believe we have our future back now," said Maya, out of nowhere, carving off a couple of chunks of Oaxaca cheese with the large pocketknife I kept in the van. You didn't often find real Oaxaca cheese in San Miguel, and the prospect of survival always put her in a better mood. She reached around from her seat in front and took Megan's hand. "Stay away from the loaves and fishes, though, OK?"

Megan gave her an ironic look. "Just show me later where the big water jugs and the wine glasses are kept." The afternoon was much in that same vein, a search for a tone less heavy.

Later that day, close to half past four as we were winding down, the question was whether to stay in

Oaxaca City or somewhere outside of it. Inside that town we'd be harder to locate, and outside more obvious in the sparse traffic when we were moving, but if we were tucked away in a more obscure place that might be the ticket. As we discussed it there was a growing sense that we'd do better out of town. We decided to stay in the same small hotel we had coming down, at La Serpiente Emplumada. We knew the place, for one thing, and we had surveyed it calmly before any danger was attached to our trip. It was small and intimate; any stranger entering the walled compound would be obvious, and we knew they secured the entrance at night. The parking was not concealed from the highway, but that was really the only problem with the place. Also, it had a laundry, a big plus for all of us whose underwear was starting to stick to our skin like Band-Aids.

"Megan, this is not a classy place we're thinking of staying in. It's clean enough, but it may not be up to your standards."

"Think where I've been staying for three months. And last night's place almost got me stoned. Let's go for it."

When we pulled in less than an hour later we found the hotel had only two rooms available, both with two beds.

"It's OK," said Megan. "I'll stay with Cody. We'll be all right. He's my dad, you know."

Cody only shrugged, but I could see he was not displeased. Maya persuaded the manager to send a maid around with a hamper to pick up all our dirty laundry. There would be no trouble telling it apart.

Feeling much more relaxed, at about six we reconvened downstairs in the courtyard for a couple of drinks. With a shower behind her and Cody beside her in the booth, Megan was glowing as if our troubled journey was finished. I didn't feel like saying this was only a halfway point, and that San Miguel at the other end was the destination that Nathan's people must feel certain we were headed for. But why wreck a party? I hadn't gotten the image of the mob out of my mind, and I didn't think the others had either. It had been like facing a savage animal that grew in size and fierceness moment by moment.

I couldn't help thinking of our last visit, barely more than a week earlier, heading blithely toward San Cristobal. What saps we'd been, believing that a simple missing person assignment carried little risk. You'd think that on our fifteenth case we would've learned to be more wary.

Maya started with a glass of cabernet, and since the pour wasn't a large one, Megan ordered one too, declaring that she would follow it with lemonade, but she needed to celebrate just a little. I felt like a couple of dark rums, and Cody ordered a planter's punch that the barman didn't know how to make, so he switched to a margarita. Three other tables were occupied and one was a bit noisy. We weren't worried about being overheard. On the second floor the rooms all faced us in the small courtyard below and none of them were lit. Dusk was just coming on.

"I'm really sorry it turned out like this," Megan said to Maya. "You must hate it when it gets so rough."

Maya gave her a modest smile, as if to say, We're all tougher than any of this. "We've all gotten used to it."

I would've backed her up by saying that Maya had killed two people in past cases, but I knew how much she hated to talk about it.

"And you were absolutely heroic this morning," Megan said to Cody. "What happens now?" She slid her hand in his direction and he seized it. Maya's lips started to curl. She had long known of Cody's interest in her, and while she had no intention of reciprocating, she never objected to having a backup admirer in the wings. I gave her an encouraging look. Soon Megan would be gone and Maya wouldn't.

"It's mainly a long drive up toward the capital tomorrow morning," Cody said, "where on the northern edge we'll pick up Highway 57 toward San Miguel. That's a little more than three hours. Then at home we kick back and decide what the next move is for you."

"I can't even think right now. A few days without being on the run, with some clean clothes and some decent meals, would put me in a better frame of mind to figure that out."

"Getting money's not a problem," said Cody. "You'll find ATMs everywhere up there."

I shouldn't have been surprised by how quickly the first round of drinks disappeared, but we ordered another. Megan stuck to her pledge of lemonade. I had another Bacardi Añejo. Cody decided to switch to wine, not liking his margarita, so he and Maya ordered a bottle of Chilean red. At the back of my mind a small voice was telling me not to relax too much, since we were still a long way from home. But in a larger sense, México is a benign place to me, and we hadn't seen the red pickup again, although I hadn't written it off. The bigger threat of the mob at San Andres had been thwarted by Cody's quick action, and I was no longer any more than marginally concerned about risk. You have to go off duty some time, and we had spent way too much time lately on duty.

"I am going to sleep very well tonight," I said, almost without meaning to. I gave Maya what I knew was a weary grin, but it was the best I could manage. She took my hand. "One of these times we are going to have a very easy case."

"And we'll even get paid at the end," she added.

A serious look clouded Megan's face. "I should warn you that my father won't be pleased when he finds out that I don't want to talk to him right now. It's not your fault, but he can be difficult when he doesn't get his way. I'm going to wait at least until after the baby is born. Somehow being pregnant is a tougher message to deliver than being a mother. Besides, I know I'm going to be far more excited to be a mother than I am being pregnant."

"Should we update him now that you're OK, or wait until we get home?" I said to her.

"Let's get there first. Until then we're not OK."

"Do you think," said Cody, "that the subtext of this case is putting you back in contact with him? More, even, than just finding you?"

She shrugged. "I haven't talked to him, of course, even though my phone is working again, but that wouldn't surprise me. I assume you got a big retainer upfront, so if there's some argument about collecting the rest…"

CHAPTER TWENTY-ONE

Perhaps we had celebrated too much. Partying can be harmful to sleep and I spent about two hours that night replaying the crowd scene at San Andres as if it had been a ballet we were staging. At about five-thirty in the morning I gave up trying to keep my eyes shut any longer and went into the bathroom and threw some water on my face, which appeared blurred in the mirror. Back in the room I paused to separate the curtains at the window overlooking the perimeter wall and the black night sky. It was again one of those occasions when I didn't know what I was seeing. It might have been a dream and I was still in bed. That would've been a good fit, since dreams mostly feature things you don't care to see. I turned back and bent over the pillows to call Maya to look at it, but she hadn't moved so I didn't wake her. She'd been having a hard time with this case and it was better to let her sleep. If what I saw was a real problem it would still be there in the morning.

On the gentle slope that rose beyond the south

wall of the hotel compound I counted between twenty-five and thirty points of light. They seemed oddly uniform, not what you would get from a scattering of distant campfires. I couldn't have said exactly why I found this troubling, but I pulled on my jeans and silently slipped out the door.

At the end of the walkway that overlooked the courtyard below, in a larger TV lounge at the front of the hotel a pair of windows overlooked the compound toward the road. Their sills started at the floor. Below, parking was provided for about a dozen cars. Between the wall and the highway beyond eight vehicles were there now, dimly lit by several security lamps on poles. On the other side of the blacktop were about twenty more lights, small and flickering. No one was moving around the row of parked cars. Third from the left was my Town and Country. Even in the imperfect light and looking down from the second floor, the van was easier to pick out than the other vehicles because a circle of lit candles surrounded it. It's become the chariot of the gods, I thought, or of the goddess, as the meaning of this grew clearer.

Even pressing my ear to the window glass, I could hear nothing from outside, no chanting, no drums. It sounded more like waiting. I couldn't see very far to the right beyond the corner of the hotel, but I had little doubt that the same thing was happening there. I went back and tapped softly on Cody and Megan's door. A muted grunt came from inside, followed by a brief pause.

"Speak or die," said Cody, in Spanish, without opening it. I knew he wasn't standing directly in front of it where I could just shoot through the center panel.

"It's Paul. Something is happening. You both need to see this."

The door swung open halfway. Behind Cody the dim glow of the bedside lamp revealed Megan adjusting her more voluminous hair after pulling her dress down over her hips. The tight curls had loosened somewhat and grown in volume again. The mass now stood higher than her head on both sides. Cody's pistol was tucked in the waistband of his pants, and he badly needed a shave. With his sleeveless tee shirt the scene was reminiscent of a passage from Tennessee Williams. I hadn't thought to bring my gun. After leaning through the door to check the scene below and to the sides, he moved out to join me and left it open for Megan.

In the lounge we stood for a long moment at the front window. Eventually she stepped between us, taking both our hands.

"I saw them from the side window too," she said. They're probably all around us now. I thought this was finished. I know I caused this, so you don't have to tell me that."

After a moment Maya took my other hand. I

hadn't heard her come out, but she must've heard us. "I see we're back between the sword and the wall," she said.

"What's it going to take to make them go away?" I said. "Another miracle?"

Megan took a while in answering. "Maybe from someone else this time."

"Don't you have any more up your sleeve?" I looked into her face. She slowly shook her head. I wondered whether she always knew the extent of her powers. Her case might be like the mother lifting the car wheel off her toddler. She's got to do it, whether she is physically able to or not. Megan might have more reserves than she knew, and we could well have need of them soon.

"Maybe we can turn the San Andres people and Nathan against each other," I said. Not a bad idea, but where was Nathan and the red pickup when we needed them?

Cody's concern that the subtext of this case might be that Megan was expected to resume contact with her father had now become irrelevant. There was no longer any subtext—everything was on the surface and in place ready to move against us. Sometimes my long suit is strategy, but here we were surrounded and outnumbered at the opening move.

My watch said the time was just approaching six o'clock. Some kitchen noises downstairs were starting up toward the back of the building.

"Let's go down there and try to set something up," said Cody. "I think this might call for the old prison laundry cart trick."

"But didn't we just have the laundry done?" said Megan, for once a little too literal-minded.

As we disengaged ourselves from the window Maya showed me her gun with a sinister smile.

"Don't take it with you in the shower," I said. She seemed in a better mood.

Cody pulled on a shirt and some shoes and we marched downstairs.

CHAPTER TWENTY-TWO
MAYA SANCHEZ

After Paul and Cody left, Maya tapped softly on Megan's door. It was not a social call, nor was it a visit she looked forward to. "It's Maya, Megan. I want to talk to you for a minute."

As she let her in, Megan was not surprised to see her. An awkward pause followed as Maya discovered she was less ready for this conversation than she thought, but she hadn't expected Paul and Cody to leave just at that moment. While she also didn't anticipate getting another opportunity for a conversation like this, she had prepared nothing to say.

"Look," Megan said, seizing the silent moment. "I know you don't like me much and you have a professional conflict because you're supposed to protect me when you wish I would just go away and leave your men alone. Both of them, and yes, I know about Cody and you."

Startled, Maya still looked at her calmly, but her

mind was racing. With a single sentence Megan had dropped it all down to the bottom line. The subject of just how attractive their client was to Paul, and secondarily, to Cody, had occupied Maya's thoughts far more than she wished since the first meeting in Mazintla. She kept telling herself that pregnant women weren't that appealing to most men, but it didn't help that many people in Chiapas had regarded Megan as a minor deity. There was also the inconvenient fact that none of this was Agency business and Maya ought to be focused on the more important things coming at them. She knew very well that you could never predict what they might be. San Andres had confirmed that.

"It is true that I haven't liked all of our clients," she replied, "but that's not the point. I don't have to like them to do my job, and I do appreciate it that you said that so frankly. Let's sit down and see if we can work this out before Paul and Cody get back."

The look that passed between them was unlike any that ever had before.

When they were settled Megan leaned back on the sofa and placed her hands on her knees. "First of all there's this. Paul Zacher is not my type, OK? I mean, he's a very talented guy and I like him, but he's too down to earth. Maybe he has to be to do this job, but when he saw what I did in that church the other night he was practically speechless. I told him that he does the same thing himself all the time with the energy that comes out of his fingers as he paints, although in a slightly different form. He struggled to see it. I know he was open to the idea, but I'm sure I didn't convince him. As for Cody, he's no less hardheaded, but he needs me in a way that Paul doesn't. He needs a daughter and he didn't know it until the moment he saw me that first night."

"Maybe you were just a little too seductive with him." Maya tried to keep her face neutral as she said this.

Megan shrugged. "Maybe I was, but it got his attention, OK? Did you ever feel desperate but you didn't want to show it because you were afraid you'd look weak?"

"No. Yes."

Megan paused and waited for Maya to add some detail, but she didn't. More than wanting to respond, she wanted to hear about Megan's perspective on her own needs. This case was not going to be settled for a while.

"Anyway, Paul looks at me as a person who is interesting mainly because of my situation in Mazintla, but beyond that he just wants to keep me out of trouble. But with Cody, I need him too. Until I met him I felt like an orphan down here, and when Leo was killed it only got worse. Cody is the first man I've known as a grownup that I could really depend on without wondering what he wanted from me. Does that make any sense to you?"

Maya got up and moved to the window. She was

surveying her own sense of boundaries with Agency clients in a way she'd never had to do before, but it did not make her want to discuss it any further. Dawn was moving in over the hilltops but in the lower areas the tiny lights were still visible, waiting in the deep shadows for Megan to make her move beyond the walls.

"Paul told me you also made him unable to see you."

"From a distance. Not from up close."

"How is that different?"

"I don't know. That's only how it works. It's all mental parlor tricks, anyway. I know I shouldn't have done it. I always think because it doesn't matter much to me that other people will see it the same way. But sometimes it's more powerful than I would like to think, at least in its effects. That's what got away from me in San Andres."

Maya looked at this statement with a degree of skepticism. "Maybe you were trying to impress Paul. Have you thought of that?" Her eyebrows went up, thinking also of how Megan had approached Cody.

Megan sighed. "Don't we all spend a lot of time trying to impress the men we know? Even when we don't want to get any closer to them? It sure never worked with my dad, though."

"Then if you're so good, at least some of the time, why don't you make them go away?" Maya pointed out the window. "They're waiting for us to come out. Don't you think they're all armed, not only with rocks this time, but with knives and guns? Clubs?"

She realized her voice was rising, but so was her frustration. Maya had easily become invested in the idea that the mob from San Andres had given up and stayed there. That the last rock sailing over the van was the final interaction they'd have. She took a deep breath, realizing she wouldn't mind offering Megan a final challenge. "Paul said you were only using willpower. Maybe that'll work now. Have them all go blind for five minutes while we drive out of here after breakfast. Cody said we can just get back on the tollway north of Oaxaca and it'll be much faster."

"I wish I could, Maya. I really do. You probably think I have much more power than I do."

A few minutes of uncomfortable silence followed. Neither of them looked at each other during most of this, nor, spinning through ideas and responses, did the either of them feel that the conversation was finished. Gradually Maya began to study her again.

"There's more, isn't there?"

Megan looked at her for a while then nodded. "I feel so guilty about leaving behind all those people who trusted me. Wouldn't you? I haven't been able to put that out of my mind."

"Absolutely."

"I feel like I led them on, like some stupid guy I was only interested in because he was driving a Corvette."

"I can imagine what you're feeling. All I can say is that you weren't in control of everything about that situation, and if Nathan hadn't made the violent choices he had, you could've gone on. You would've found someone, in time, to join you and if you'd wanted to move on, at least there would've been a successor to minister to those people you attracted."

"Thanks for that. You're making sense, but I can't get rid of the image of them in that church with an empty pulpit."

"I'll just say this. To me, religion, or spirituality, if you want to think of it like that, if it exists at all, it's in everyone's heart, yours and theirs. They will find their own access to it, just as you do." A moment of silence followed, then Maya rose and put her arms around Megan. "I have an idea. Tell me more about how you got that awful muumuu." Maya didn't have to point.

"It was a gift from a woman in my congregation, several women, I think. They made it. A group of them took a special interest in me because I was pregnant."

"But at the same time you know that's not a style any pregnant Mexican woman would wear. They would always prefer a snug top above jeans that expand at the waist, something like that. Those women that gave it to you would've known that too, even out there as far away from civilization as Mazintla."

"I know. I saw a lot of that in San Cris because I was looking at the way pregnant women dressed. I think what the church ladies were really trying to do was cover me up more during the services, and they knew I couldn't get any other clothes there that weren't handmade. I'm sure they thought my airy skirt was way too revealing, but it was meant to be. I made it from a curtain on the second floor of the parish house, one I found in the spare bedroom. Pulling it down and making it into a skirt, I felt a little bit like Scarlett O'Hara. You remember the scene where she makes a whole dress out of some draperies."

Maya had never read or seen *Gone with the Wind*, but she understood the concept. "But you're not deeply attached to that muumuu, are you?"

"Only that it's comfortable now, at a time when nothing much else is. I know that as a maternity style it sucks. But I was making my own fashion statement there, too. You saw that." She picked up the hem of the skirt, studied it for a moment, and dropped it back on her knees. "The stitching is really good, though. It's all done by hand since there was no electricity."

"Our laundry will be coming back up in a bit, I think. You'll have your blue skirt to wear again, clean now. We'll all have clean underwear."

"That's my dream." Megan paused as a shocked

look came over her face.

"What is it?"

"I *did* have a dream. It was so horrible! About the baby. It was a boy just as I thought, and Brother Nathan had it. I came into the nursery somewhere—I don't know where it was—not Mazintla—and he was lifting it out of the crib with one hand, and a horrible grin on his face. He had the baby's wrists together in his hand." Her eyes wide with horror, she pressed her hands over her mouth.

Maya wrapped her arms around Megan for a long moment. Not for the first time, she found herself wondering whether she and Paul would ever have a baby. This was followed immediately by another thought.

"I'd like to use this muumuu to get us out of here alive," she said softly.

Megan looked back at her for a moment. "That's an even better idea than wearing it. It's yours."

CHAPTER TWENTY-THREE

Plutarco Gomez was the owner of our small hotel near the Oaxaca airport, La Serpiente Emplumada, and we had met him briefly on the way down from San Miguel. He had told us before that his patriotic father and grandfather had owned it before him, and he was committed to carrying on their mission. The bougainvillea that draped the inner courtyard walls was sixty years old and still flourishing.

He was a cordial *patrón* with dark curly hair, broad chested but not tall, with a mustache big enough for the upper lip of a Mexican revolutionary hero. We had reminded him coming in of our earlier stay not long before. Of course he remembered us. His easy manner made him a natural for the hospitality business.

Cody and I left Maya and Megan to take showers while we went downstairs and tried to work out a way of getting back on the road without being killed or captured. What we had on our side was that the mob from San Andres did not know where in Guanajuato we were going. Naturally they had seen our state license plates when we loaded at the hotel. They could always guess it was San Miguel, but it would be no more than that. Unlike Nathan, they were poor and probably had little money to devote to our pursuit. To me it seemed like we only had to outlast them until they ran out of gas money.

Plutarco Gomez guided us through his office into a back room that must have been part of his residence. Fitted with a small flat screen TV and *equipale* furniture, it looked out on a flower-filled courtyard in back that wasn't visible from the public areas of the hotel. From the sounds of the prep cooking I heard it must have been adjacent to the kitchen. With his broad, gracious smile, it would've been easy to roll a ten-peso coin on edge through the gap in his upper teeth when he offered us a seat at the round table. An older woman rushed forward to wipe off the surface, although it appeared to be clean already.

"I hope you're having the start of a great day," Cody said for openers, "but we are already in trouble."

This was met by a profound shrug that expressed compassion more than indifference. "And which of us is not, my friend?" said Gomez. "It is a world most difficult at times, but we have no other. It is also a world that can offer some cures. Please tell me your problem."

"Traveling with us is a young woman who is…"

"Ah, *sí*. She is *embarazada*." This is the rather nuanced Mexican word for pregnant.

"Her *novio* (fiancé)," I added, "was murdered in Chiapas before their wedding had a chance to take place. So, as you can see, we have taken responsibility for her welfare as she travels home to be with her family."

"A noble act. And her family lives in México?"

"No, they live in Minnesota," I said.

"Ah! A part of Canada, I think, no?"

"Yes, a good deal of the time."

"Rosario! Bring us some coffee. How can I help you? Or her?"

"Well," said Cody, "from across the line in Chiapas she has attracted a following that believes she has magical powers. I can't imagine why they would think that."

Gomez responded with a benign chuckle that was not without a hint of cynicism. "Excuse me, but I think if she had magical powers she would not have found herself *embarazada* without a husband."

"This is true."

"So that was her following placing the candles all around that I saw this morning as I opened the gate?"

"Yes."

"Then there are many of them. I thought they were the teachers from the city making trouble again."

"Not this time," I said. "We need to find a way to get her out of here without them seeing her. They believe we are keeping her from them, so they hate us."

A young woman came out of the kitchen and put down some small plates, a large platter of papaya slices with lime, and a ceramic pot of coffee.

"You are thinking of doing something about it today?" Gomez said, pouring us each a cup.

"If that is possible," Cody said. "For example, if there is a delivery truck coming this morning?" This was the prison laundry solution, where you stuffed the escapee in the laundry bin and he was rolled out through the door by trusted people from outside the walls. It was a B movie cliché, but it might still fly in Oaxaca.

"I am expecting two. The first one brings fruits and vegetables from the *campesinos*. The other comes later from the creamery, so it is chilled fot the milk and cheeses."

"Is the first one an open truck or is it also closed?"

"Closed, because it is often used to carry furniture and household goods for the people moving."

Cody gave me a hopeful look. "Could it hold four people and a suitcase?"

Plutarco Gomez shrugged. "Who can say? You could see it for yourself at about seven-thirty when he arrives. What would happen to your van then, if you should depart in that way?"

"We would have to leave it here," I said. "Then come back for it once we got the young lady to a safe place. It wouldn't take long. Do you think the produce driver would help us?" The idea of leaving the van behind again gave me a queasy feeling. I didn't want to leave Maya behind to bring it at some distance after us because then they'd all follow her.

"You would have to persuade him a little, I think." Gomez' thumb and forefinger came up and massaged each other expressively.

At that moment Maya and Megan walked in. As if it was a trophy, Maya was carrying the folded up muumuu. Cody introduced them to Plutarco Gomez. Rosario must have been watching because she brought two fresh cups and more coffee. I told them about the truck escape idea.

"We had the same thought," said Maya, "except with one more wrinkle—that none of us would really be on the truck. It would only be this muumuu, and it would stick out the back a few inches as if Megan had jumped on in a hurry and closed the door on it. That way after everyone takes off down the road following it, we would just get in the van and head for home like normal."

And what was normal? I thought. "Would they fall for anything so simple?" I said.

"Of course. They are blinded by the light," said Megan.

"I am liking this idea so much better now," said Plutarco. "This way when the followers catch up with the driver he can say he had no idea that this was caught in his back door. How could he know? There would be no chases through the streets of the city where the burros and small children can be killed. Then he can go about his business."

"And then he can also turn over my dress to them to be cut up into small relics and handed out to commemorate my saintly visit to their village," said Megan with no trace of smugness. She sipped her coffee with a satisfied look, picturing this, I imagine.

Maya gave her a glance that suggested she might still be too full of herself.

"I'm not joking," Megan said. "There was an older guy in my congregation who wanted me to save my finger and toenail clippings for him. He said he had a little altar at home."

"I wonder if that was really about religion?" said Maya, "Or something else."

Plutarco stared at Megan with what I hoped was not a blissfully admiring look, but I didn't know him well enough to be sure. Maybe it was the same facial expression he used to keep his guests coming back, but I still wondered if he was drifting over into her follower's camp even as we sat there. We needed to shut down the divine Megan Anderson and soon.

CHAPTER TWENTY-FOUR
MAYA SANCHEZ

It was standard practice with the Paul Zacher Agency that when they wished to launch a successful negotiation with a Mexican man they sent an attractive Mexican woman to cut the deal. That was the simple geometry of it, and some things you just don't experiment with. Back in San Miguel Maya would've dressed in a short black skirt and a silk blouse with suitable cleavage, strappy shoes, and gone out to meet her hapless victim. After minoring in flirting in college (with highest honors), she had kept her skills intact through frequent practice over the years. On this Chiapas trip they hadn't anticipated any negotiations, so she didn't have the perfect flirtation outfit with her. She had to improvise that part of the set up, but her body language would be dependably eloquent, regardless of the ensemble.

Behind the kitchen a loading area was screened from the private garden and walled off from the rest of the grounds. A pair of once-painted steel doors at the back provided access for one small truck at a time. At 7:35 Rosario opened the kitchen door and signaled to Maya that the produce delivery truck had arrived. Dressed in her usual spray on jeans, now freshly laundered, and a snug white ribbed cotton top with a generously scooped neckline, she was ready. Unfortunately this ensemble provided no space to conceal anything thicker than a theater ticket, to say nothing of a gun, but given that her opponent in this negotiation was neutral and unprepared, she didn't feel she needed one. Furthermore, she thought as she walked through the kitchen, she would have no need of any cheesy magic tricks of the Edina earth goddess variety to bring this off. It was the kind of venture where the age-old fundamentals of gender dynamics would work just fine.

The produce truck was a well-used blue Dodge that had probably begun life as a pickup in the late nineties, but now had a larger cargo box grafted onto that chassis. It had no refrigeration unit, so it would be confined to short-run local deliveries. Since the growers in the Oaxaca Valley were an informal group, no company logo branded the sides. As Maya closed the door to the kitchen storage area behind her, she was surprised to see that the driver was still sitting in the cab, rather than unloading at the back. He appeared to be scanning a clipboard when he looked up at her in mild surprise and offered a quick but tentative smile that made her think for a moment he might have been expecting someone else.

She also had a sudden impression that she had seen this man before, but she put it aside, since that was extremely unlikely. Wearing a worn pair of cargo pants and a pale green beer company jacket, he stepped out of the cab as she came around to the side of the truck. Immediately she did not like his expression. She could read the nuance of it as clearly as a road sign. As a driver on a rural delivery route in Oaxaca he should've been much more deferential to a woman with as much urban polish as Maya always displayed. The pale tone of her skin alone would have told him how to act.

At the same time his gestures and posture were more humble, as if he was a person of no account recently raised to a position of unaccustomed power. But what would that be? None of this looked right, none of it made sense. She had an opening line prepared, but observing this, she held it back, waiting for him to speak.

"I'm looking for someone who is staying here," he said. "I have something for her."

Maya glanced at the truck. This was not what she expected. "Don't you have fruits and vegetables for the hotel?"

"Yes, but I was told I have to do this first." The original game is over, thought Maya, and this is now something else. She wanted to look back to see if anyone was watching this from inside, like Paul or Cody, but she didn't want to suggest to this driver that anyone else might be there.

"What is her name?"

The man shook his head slightly. "I was only given her description, because I was told it would be easy to find her here. She is an American, a *güera* (blonde) of a height like yours, and she is *embarazada*. I have a package for her in the back. Perhaps it is a gift for her baby."

"What about the vegetables and fruits? What stops you from doing that? The hotel owner is waiting." And looking out the window to watch this fiasco, she hoped.

"After I give her this package I can unload them. It has to come off first, since it blocks the way for the rest." The man shifted from one foot to the other, waiting, looking at the ground. "Perhaps you could ask her to come out now."

Not believing the package could be that big, if it existed at all, Maya studied him for a moment. "If you will unload it, I can take the package for her. *La güera* has the room next to mine. Then you can unload the produce and go on about your business. You must be late for your other stops now."

"Yes." The deliveryman looked like he had outrun the limit of his prepared dialog and found himself in the land of improvisation, foreign terrain.

When he added nothing more, Maya continued. "What is in the package?"

"I think it must be clothing, just from the weight."

Good guess, thought Maya. That goddess woman dresses like an urchin when she bothers to dress at all. Still, an unexpected flicker of sympathy for Megan's understandable wardrobe deficiencies came over her at this point, but she set it aside. The man in front of her was shrinking in size, looking less formidable with every moment that passed.

A sudden thought came to her. This could not be the original driver. Where was he? Rosario and Plutarco Gomez would both know him by sight. What legitimate business could this man have with Megan? Worse, far worse, how could he even know she was there? Maya strained to catch any sound from behind her. She heard nothing, so she made the only move she could think of. She needed more information.

"Open the back door and show me this package now. I can't decide until I see it." She walked around to the back of the truck and waited, arms folded over her chest, which now felt too prominent and exposed. A seductive presentation was not going to settle any of this.

After a long unrewarding moment the driver appeared. With both hands in his pockets, not a normal Mexican manner, he was clearly nervous. Maya used an old device that usually gave her courage in a tough spot.

She imagined her footprints on his back.

"Open this door now. What are you waiting for? I don't believe you have any packages in there, aside from fruits and vegetables. Show it to me now if you do."

He didn't move any further.

"So, you don't really have it? What is your name, *joven?*" Giving orders was easier if you knew that. Anyone's name could be pronounced like an insult. *Joven* was the way she would address a waiter in a restaurant. It meant kid, or boy. "Who is your boss? I don't think you're doing your job here. I'm going to give him a call." Maya's imperious tone was one she didn't use herself, but she had heard it often enough among the female customers from Mexico City in the Mega supermarket who were spending the weekend in San Miguel. The driver couldn't summon a rational response.

Maya's eyes strayed over the fastening on the doors. It was only a latch, where a thick steel lever on a pin dropped into a U-shaped bracket. Since the paired doors overlapped, gravity held them locked, at least from inside. Thinking of Cody's manner with the mob in front of the hotel in San Andres, she took a large step toward the driver. Unprepared for this, he recoiled two steps. Maya turned, lifted the latch with a confident gesture, and flipped the doors open.

The real driver inside was just wriggling out of the rope that bound his wrists.

CHAPTER TWENTY-FIVE

Oddly, it was the original plan that we ended up using. Usually you have to modify them to gain any traction at all when the real game begins. Maya's shout at seeing the original driver get up from the box untied brought us all outside. The phony driver had nowhere to run to, but he tried to anyway, and she took the precaution of tripping him as he passed her. We were already in motion and all I had to do was pick him up.

A little of Cody's persuasive interrogation style told us the story. All the lights on the hillside that night and morning had been, as we thought, from Megan's new San Andres fan club. Keeping a distance, they had followed us into Oaxaca. If this was too reminiscent of the red pickup, it did illustrate the power of religion, or what looked like religion, to some people. I decided I needed to have another talk with Megan about that once we got settled.

We did not have to bribe the real driver to place a

substantial fringe of Megan's muumuu sticking out from the back doors of the truck as he left, since the chief benefit for him in this exchange was what he could sell the cut up squares of Megan's muumuu for once he stopped. The rest was safe inside the truck. Gomez even loaned him a pair of scissors. I don't think the driver had any real idea of the game we were playing, but freedom is a great persuader, and he bought into it. Naturally, he would have to explain to the San Andres people what happened to their man, but they had waylaid him as well, so it might be an interesting conversation between two sets of victims where he held the fabric goods that gave him the upper hand. Gleefully, we had no intention of being there to see this transaction.

The cash came out during the conversation with Plutarco Gomez that followed, but he treated us gently on the issue of how long he would hold the fake driver. We agreed on twenty-four hours in exchange for 2,400 pesos. I guess you might call it kidnapping, but since the fake driver had been involved in snatching the original driver, it seemed like a fair trade off. No one was likely to mention it after his release tomorrow.

We were on the road soon after that crowd moved on as they passed in solemn formation behind Megan's green muumuu. We waited for only five minutes after the caravan of cars was out of sight to depart ourselves.

No one complained that the road home seemed oddly anticlimactic. Four and a half hours later even the traffic around Mexico City seemed benign. No one tried to kill us except by rear end impact. Several times Maya tried to steer the conversation toward what Megan thought she wanted to do next, but the former cult goddess had not made up her mind. No one brought it up, but there was ample time, since as long as the red pickup had not yet appeared, we all felt there had to be another shoe ready to drop.

At 4:30 that afternoon, home looked better than it ever had. Our housekeeper, Rigoberta, who had been with me since before Maya, had everything in prime condition. She had seen no suspicious activity around the house or along Quebrada, our street. I barricaded the entry door that first night and the following morning the locksmith arrived to change the lock while we were just finishing breakfast.

Without the required bi-weekly treatment, within three days of leaving Mazintla, Megan's hair had relaxed enough to resemble a blond Afro with about double the volume of the previous do. It was not her best look, but she assured us that soon it would return to its normal thick, straight appearance. I didn't think she looked any bigger, but she was clearly less comfortable, walking with a bit more of a waddle and leaning against things when she could.

Two days passed and we were more relaxed than we'd been since we first glimpsed the road going into Mazintla. Maya, whose optimism tended to revive faster than mine or Cody's, even started to comment that the case might be over. Maybe Nathan and his crew had given up, since it wasn't worth it to them to traipse all over the country.

I smiled, but at that instant I again recalled giving the Agency business card to the hammock house manager. Possibly nothing would come of that, so I decided not to mention it. Why have people losing any sleep over it? We were a long way from Chiapas, and this was our own turf. Anyway, they'd gotten their church back, unless Megan's congregation had decided to fight it out in her absence. If Brother Nathan thought that in coming up this way he would find God was on his side in San Miguel too, he had a lesson to learn. We have our share of zealots here among the expats, but they're mostly political, not religious.

After two days, having Megan as a houseguest wasn't going that well. I know Cody would've preferred to have her stay with him, but he only had one bedroom. Maya was already tired of having her around, and her natural Mexican sense of hospitality was at odds with her desire to return to our normal life without boarders. She planned to start disappearing four hours a day riding. Still, we all felt that there might well be another chapter to this story, and we didn't want to expose Megan to any more violence without our support.

It had started poorly that morning of the second day after our return. Megan met us in the chilly kitchen at about seven-thirty. I was just pouring some coffee. She looked a little blurry and somewhat clumsy, still trying to get her bearings in a strange place. She was wearing a new pink cotton nightshirt that came to eight inches above her knees, and blue flip-flops. The shirt had a lot of stretch and bulged out comfortably over her abdomen. Maya had taken her shopping the day after we got in, while Cody rode shotgun outside the stores in La Luciernaga, our mall on the edge of town. Maya handed her an old robe as she sat down.

"Thank you for that," she said, "and getting me here, too. Even if I haven't figured out what comes next, somehow I don't think they can find me now."

I probably should've responded to that, but I didn't want to alarm her. We sat at the tiled counter in the kitchen, since the morning was too cold to sit outside for breakfast. Maya hadn't said much but was trying to study Megan without seeming to.

"Do you need anything more?" she said with an overly formal smile.

"I don't think so. Thanks for putting out that yellow toothbrush for me. I lost mine on the trip somehow."

"That's the dog's toothbrush," Maya said.

Megan nearly spit out her coffee.

Now it's starting, I thought. "We don't have a dog, Megan, we never have. That's just part of Maya's welcoming ritual. She's a great kidder. We got that toothbrush at the hotel in San Cristobal. It's brand new." I shot Maya a look but she wasn't receiving. She turned around and went back upstairs. An hour later she left for Rancho Camarena.

I took care of some Agency business at our workstation in the great room, and afterward went out to the garden in search of Megan to see if she needed anything. The morning had warmed considerably. It was about 11:30.

She was sitting in the loggia at the edge of the garden. As if she had drifted away in her mind, she wore a pensive look. I was certain she was taking advantage of this quiet time, the first since Mazintla, to reexamine the whole episode back in Chiapas. I sat across and down from her at that long table where we ate most of our meals in good weather. To her left was an empty glass with the dregs of some lemonade, and halfway between us was an ordinary stainless steel spoon. Her hand crept forward and stopped about a foot and a half from it; the limit of her reach without bending over the table or getting to her feet. Two rigid fingers of her right hand pointed at the handle. The spoon started moving toward her, minutely at first, no faster than thread by thread across the coarse, hand-woven tablecloth. I tried to catch her eye but she wouldn't look back at me. Her face held no look of triumph, it only seemed a little tired even through her concentration.

So here it comes again, I thought. These skills are like a refuge for her. She's feeling powerless here, at our mercy, and exiled in a strange town without a plan. She needs to do this to demonstrate she's still in control of something in her life. Still, these tricks can't be that hard, either. At least no one else can see her doing this.

Frowning, I focused my mind on that spoon, boring into it like a laser, thinking I was getting inside its molecular structure. I could almost feel the metal penetrate my fingers, fuse with my fleshy cells. I tried to make it both warmer and then cooler as I bent it to my will. All I wanted was to stop the movement she was causing, and perhaps a little more. It was probably all in my mind, but wasn't that where it came from with her too? Thinking I had achieved the first step, I next visualized the spoon reversing direction and moving back toward me. Did it tremble for an instant with indecision? Perhaps, but I still couldn't stop it from creeping toward her.

To see if it felt hot or electrically charged I covered it with my hand. It kept moving. I gripped the handle and found I couldn't lift it or even retard its minuscule progress in any way. The spoon's passage across the table did not change at all.

"I give up," I said, looking at her. Megan smiled at me, not a cordial smile, but one more like triumphant. Not evil, certainly, but not exactly benign, either. More like simply forceful and commanding. I turned away. She certainly had some uncommon skills about her, but I didn't believe they were magical. I had seen most of these wiles before, and plenty of people had them. While I could not have put a name to them, parlor tricks still did not do them justice.

"What is this power, really?" I said. "You always try to diminish its significance, as if everyone can do it, but that's not the case. I tried just now. I gave it every-thing I had and I couldn't even lift that spoon off the table. You controlled it completely."

She shook her head. "You're only lacking in experience, Paul. Try it some time when you're alone, when you're not performing for anybody, and failure doesn't matter. You might surprise yourself with what you can do when no one is looking."

I leaned toward her, feeling like she was making excuses for me. "I am never afraid of failure. I take risks all the time in my painting where everyone can see it. I attempt things I have no idea whether I can pull off. Stumbling doesn't bother me. That's how I've always learned. But most of all, in the Agency, the price of my failure is death, either for me or for one of the others." I pulled back, surprised at my own vehemence. She didn't respond to this. "What if I was able to do it too," I continued in a calmer tone, "and we went head to head over that spoon. Who would win?"

"I would because I have more practice."

"Is practice what it takes to get it?"

"No, I just discovered it accidentally one day. I only meant that I've done it a lot, and it does get stronger over time. That's why you couldn't lift it off the table."

"Could you lift this table without touching it?"

"I don't think so. Maybe one of the benches just a little, like at one end."

I thought of the person Megan had been with her congregation, and who she was now. Maybe there was no difference. Later, the mob in San Andres had been convinced she was a saint. "And is this all there is?"

"What do you mean?"

"I'm thinking of you doing things like this in Mazintla. You said that it was a way to get your congregation to listen, but how does this connect to morals, or to ethics? Isn't that why you were down there? You hear a lot in religion, almost any religion, about forgiveness, about redemption from the bad acts we do. Are we redeemed by moving spoons or lighting candles without matches? I'm not just talking about in a religious way, because I'm not religious, but are we redeemed in any other way? How does it help us? Does it move us forward or make us better people?"

She only shook her head, as if I'd moved off topic.

"If I ever went to church it would be because I was looking for guidance," I added.

"That goes way beyond these parlor tricks. You must know that. I'm the wrong person to ask a question like that."

"But you talked in Chiapas about kindness and consideration for other people, so isn't it still about morality in some way?"

"No! It's only a church. You're not getting it." Her voice was starting to sound irritated.

I looked at her for a long moment, still very far from understanding her. "Well, that's all still out there, though, somewhere, and every church I've ever seen has been selling some variety of it. Let me ask you a question. You said some harsh things about your father that first night we met you. They seemed heartfelt. If you got a message from your mother saying he was dying, would you go back to Minnesota now to say goodbye? Would you forgive him?"

Putting her fingers to her lips she looked into the garden for a while with a sigh, perhaps examining our banana tree with its huge sinister black and purple flower. Her face looked vaguely uncomfortable; it was something at the corners of her eyes.

"Do you think my father would ever apologize to

me? You met him. Would he ever ask my forgiveness for the things he did to me? I haven't told you all of them by any means. If he didn't ask forgiveness, wouldn't it be a terrible sham for me to be standing there at his bedside at the end? Wouldn't it be utterly phony for both of us? How could that be redemption for anyone? Forgiveness is easy to talk about, but not so easily done. Worse, it's not so easily asked for, either."

It was my turn to look away. I stuck my hands in my pockets because I didn't know what else to do with them. "It might make him happy. I know that's not the same as redemption."

We didn't discuss these issues much in the Agency; we usually operated closer to the ground than that. It didn't take Megan long to respond.

"Make him happy to have it swept under the rug again, and for the final time? If it didn't make him happy it would certainly make him relieved. Maybe that's enough. Or what if he didn't feel any guilt at all? What if he had always rationalized what he did to other people? That's what most of us do. I can see why you'd ask that question. You must come up against these issues all the time. Cody said all of you had killed people doing Agency business. Obviously people have tried to kill you. Has anyone ever apologized to you for the evil things they did to you, or tried to do? Anyone in your entire life? People who would have sworn they loved you?" She leaned forward as she said this, and the strange deteriorating but still uplifted hairdo of the Mazintla women gave her an almost demonic look. Shaking my head, I suddenly recalled her blackened eye sockets the night we met her.

"No. That has never happened to me." I had never thought of it in those terms before, either. I didn't anyone to ever apologize to me. I looked at Jalanme'tik ta Banomil thinking that I had never really thought of her in that way before. Goddesses don't have to ask forgiveness for what they do, and maybe they can dispense forgiveness even when it's not requested.

"There is still that question," I said. "What about morality and redemption? Where was that in your mission, if that was what you called it?"

Megan looked at me as if I was pushing too hard. Maybe I was. "That was never a part of it," she said. "That *wasn't* my mission, and that was beyond the boundaries of it. You need to look into your own heart for that. Everybody does. It's a gift that cannot be given, OK? Any church that claims to offer that is only lying to you as they pass around the collection plate."

"Religion," I said. "Then perhaps it's all just anthropology. It must've been a good fit for you." From out on Quebrada a sound truck passed blaring its gibberish message in high volume, Spanish so rapid and distorted I could barely make it out. The clearest part was *solo veinte pesos! Solo veinte pesos!* Only twenty pesos, a dollar and twenty cents. A moment later the message was gone on the breeze, fading in the way a siren winds out on a thread, and the moment had passed.

And who are you then, Megan?

Did I really say that? I thought for a moment that I did, but she hadn't noticed. Maybe the lingering noise had drowned out my voice.

Megan Anderson offered me nothing more. I wondered if I had always expected too much from her, from the moment I first saw her as the goddess in that isolated church. Maybe she had developed no further insight into these questions herself, and had given me all she knew about it. Was that why she had kept her message light and upbeat in that old village church in Mazintla? Some things can't be explained. Maybe her parlor tricks were only a fragment of a force like gravity, a ten-cent amusement, a trivial part of a power larger than they seemed in themselves. The spoon still lay on the table between us, now still. That's all there was, but I couldn't let it go. I seized her hand for a moment. It was limp and unresisting. No electrical charge came from it, no muscular tension, no magic or parlor tricks. No emotion. No welcome.

Did pushing a spoon along the tabletop without touching it have its own meaning and gravitas? We are physically attracted to the earth and the earth to us. We walk around on it, we fall on it when we trip, but we don't think about it much and we can never understand how it really works, how two objects of such disparate size can be irresistibly drawn to each other. Yet, it is a part of every single movement we make, even breathing. So is morality, but that's easier to forget, and it can be ignored in a way that gravity cannot. It's less insistent.

These were questions Megan was not asking herself.

Did Brother Nathan possess some special capabilities too? If he had killed Leo, and that wasn't his first murder, then moral insight wasn't one of them. He would've needed those gifts far more than Megan did, with her natural magnetism. I had felt her attraction in that way more than once. It was not sexual, but it was a powerful draw nonetheless, more like the slow, insistent pull of gravity. Still, I had to wonder how deep her repertory of skills went.

"What did you take away from your Mazintla experience?" During this pause I had struggled for an extended moment to clear my voice of emotion.

She looked at me with her lips slightly pursed, her fingers working at the fabric of the tablecloth.

"Do you really want to know? It may not be what you think if you're looking for something profound."

"That's why I asked. Consider what we went through to get you out of Chiapas. That was no walk in the park for any of us."

She nodded slowly, as if she had thought long and hard about this but had never said it aloud before. "I came away with the realization that I never want to have that much responsibility for so many people again."

"One is going to be a better number," I said, nodding.

"Exactly. That's all I'm ready to handle right now." She placed her hands on her abdomen. "I'm also really tired. I need to get my energy back for what's coming."

I wondered if she was talking about the baby.

CHAPTER TWENTY-SIX

The following morning after breakfast I walked downtown to retrieve our mail at Caravan, a company that drives it down from an address in Laredo twice a week as they also bring up a load of local letters bearing U.S. stamps. For expats who don't wish to depend on the Mexican mail service it's always handy, especially if they only spend part of the year here. Maya and I use both systems.

It was a bright crisp day in December, the kind that ends up in the high seventies or low eighties by mid afternoon once the morning clouds clear out. Rain is rare. The days are short but they usually bloom in the afternoon. Planting season in San Miguel starts on Candelaria, February 2, or Groundhog Day in the States. I was happy to be doing something that felt normal again, although we hadn't dropped our guard much.

Maya had taken the van out to Rancho Camarena to ride again. I didn't expect to see much of her until we got Megan settled elsewhere. The previous night we had talked about Megan for a while at bedtime, and we both felt the case was winding down. Maya was not surprised that Megan had been unable to offer much in the area of ethics or morals. Maya mainly wanted her normal life back and I was ready to start painting again. For her at least, riding meant getting out of the house and the constant reminder that our latest case had turned into a long session of babysitting. After a case was finished it was sometimes difficult to pick up a brush again and be truly engaged. I could see the need at some point not far off to make a decision about whether Brother Nathan was coming after us again or not.

On the way home I climbed the stairs from Calle Canal to the Quebrada overpass. The sun had come out early and it promised to be a warm day.

As I walked down half a block and across the street toward the house, I saw something shining on the cobblestones between two cars. Mexican coins are not usually bright unless they're quite new, but I walked over to look at it anyway. I'm not above picking up free money. What I was astonished to find instead was my own key ring, with its chrome medallion and the van key and house key on it. But it was our *old* house key. The one that no longer worked since I'd had the lock changed within sixteen hours of our return from Chiapas. This was the key ring I had last seen when we dropped off the van at El Toro Verde above Ocosingo. The one I had naively placed in the hand of the faithless cantina owner. The same one that must have been thrown into the street here in exasperation when Nathan's entourage found it wouldn't work anymore in getting them into my house. Half a second later I was running flat out to my front door.

Nathan may even have seen me leave the house that morning. They may have been watching us for the patterns of our lifestyle over the past three days. If they hadn't gotten inside through the front entry, then they might now be trying to come over the walls, entering through some neighbor's house further down the row. As with most of this city, most of the buildings on this block share common walls, and in some places it's possible to cross from one to another, whether up or down, if you can get to the adjacent level. If they'd been able to force their way into the block through a different house, they could be inside mine now. Was Megan even still alive? How had we gone through all of that only to lose her on our own turf at the end?

As I ran I was foolishly thinking about how several times Maya and I had discussed whether we wanted to add a fence with spikes on it at the top of the parapet for extra security, but we both felt that would keep out only the casual intruders, not the determined ones. We always kept the bedroom and studio doors locked on the second floor terrace in back, but there were stairs that went on down to the garden, where we kept the doors on that level locked at night too. Now Megan was home alone and if she was outside they could get at her. I had cautioned her not to open the front door, or even respond to a ring in any way.

I was wearing my gun under a loose-fitting shirt. All three us in the Agency had been armed ever since our return. Megan still had the small revolver we'd taken from El Toro Verde. I wasn't sure how much it was worth in her hands or what she'd be willing to do with it. Now I was probably going to find out.

The stiff new entry lock resisted the key for a moment, but then I burst through forgetting silence, my heart pounding like an executioner's drumroll against my ribs, the gun ready in my hand. Dropping the mail to the floor, I sprinted through the *zaguan*, seeing no one as I glanced into the great room and then the kitchen in passing. I charged out through the corridor exit to the edge of the garden and froze.

And there was Brother Nathan, the migrant killer inspired by his wrathful god, draped in his sinister black monk's cowl, advancing toward the loggia carrying a long knife in his hand with a ceremonial step and a wickedly righteous grin. Megan had said he would want to disembowel her like a biblical sacrifice. From the corner of my eye I thought I glimpsed her clasped hands come up as she sat at the table, but I was already drawing a bead on the cult leader's head. At about a dozen meters away it was not an easy shot. He was so focused on Megan that I don't think he noticed me emerge from the house. In any case, I couldn't let him get any closer to her before I pulled the trigger.

His grotesque yell of triumph was cut off as I fired the .38 revolver twice. He staggered backward and fell on his left side. The impact of the shots echoed for a moment beyond the loggia. Megan stood up shakily and leaned forward to look at him over the far edge of the table as I rushed up next to her. Both her hands gripped the pistol as it still pointed at Nathan's body. "Put the gun down," I said softly, touching her shoulder with my fingertips. "It's over now."

I went around to the other side and bent over Nathan. He was lying unmoving on his back. One bullet had passed through the fleshy part of his neck and exited with a larger ragged hole further around on the left side under his ear. I had hit him once. It was not a fatal shot, since the small amount of blood told me it had missed an artery as it passed in front of his spine. But in the center of his forehead was another entry wound, a perfect lesser hole that must have come from Megan's beat up old pistol. It was the kind of small bore round that, after passing once through bone on entering, lacked the momentum to exit through another layer of the skull, so it simply bounced around several times, carving a randomly lethal ricochet path inside the brain. This one must have been simultaneous with my first shot, because I hadn't heard it. My second shot had probably ended somewhere in the bromeliads, passing over him as Nathan started to fall.

I bent over him but could find no pulse in his neck or wrist, and the blood flow had stopped. Brother Nathan had gone to meet his maker, whoever or wherever he believed that might be. What would he have said at the end, if he could've said anything, knowing he had a moment to live? The same cant he fed his disciples, or a meaningful final statement?

Megan moved around next to me and I stood up and put my arms around her.

"Good job," I said, close to her ear. "That was a cool hand when he was coming at you like that."

"Did I kill him? Did I really do that?" Her voice was low and breathy, and at first her hands were shaking, but even as we stood there she gradually relaxed.

"Yes. He found his own martyrdom, since he must have seen you point that gun at him. I wonder if he thought he was bulletproof."

"But how easy that was," she said sadly. "How shocking." She pressed both fists together under her chin and lowered her head against my shoulder.

"It could just as well have been you lying there, Megan."

The design of the knife lying next to Nathan's

body on the limestone pavers looked Middle Eastern. It may have been an antique Ottoman piece, with a long curved blade, an elaborately worked handle done in silver wire, leather strips, and semiprecious stones. It was a ceremonial design, one that would fit well with Megan being a sacrifice of sorts. As I would with any weapon, I released her and kicked it several feet away from the dead man's hand.

The expression on her face was now calm and less emotional. Apparently her special skills hadn't been much help here. "Couldn't you have made him unable to see you?" I said. "Like when he came down the steps he was far enough away for that to work, wasn't he?"

Her face showed no reaction to this idea. "Yes, I suppose I could have, but more than that I wanted this to be over. For weeks, long before you came to Mazintla, I've been waiting for this moment, knowing it was approaching, because otherwise, there would've come a time when it was me who didn't see him." She gave me a direct, unblinking look. "You can understand, I think, how it was always going to be one of us that killed the other."

"You said once it would've ended with your being his slave."

"It might have started that way, but it was always going to end this way, for one of us."

"I suppose that became clear the day Leo

disappeared."

"Right. I can't see anything in the future, but I did see that this was inevitable. On the drive up here I even imagined it happening inside your house, even though I had no idea what this place looked like."

There was no way to second-guess this. I could see no space in which to insert any ideas about morality from our conversation of the day before. I was still studying her face when suddenly I caught a subtle scraping sound from the upper terrace. Megan and I should've been the only people in the house. This was not finished. Brother Nathan had come in with some muscle. This made sense, because he was a short man and the parapets would've been challenging for him without someone to help him over.

I didn't know how many more people were up there, but I did know I still had four rounds in my gun when I hit the steps running up to the second floor terrace, taking three at a time. That sound had to be from our deck furniture being shoved against the common wall on the level above that. The parapet between us and the neighbor's house stood a little more than seven feet over our third floor deck. While it was an easy drop from the other side, no one could reach it to leave our terrace without standing on something. I got to the top of the steps in five strides and leaped onto the next set. I was halfway to the third floor terrace when I saw one man.

The intruder was taller than Nathan by five or six inches, dressed in a dark red checked flannel shirt and battered jeans. He had taken an old sun-bleached teak table where Maya and I sometimes had dinner on mild evenings and shoved it against the base of the wall. He already had his arms over the parapet, and his shirt had pulled up to reveal a gun in his belt. I paused long enough to fire a round into the stucco inches from his face. He was momentarily blinded when the splatter of plaster dust and fragments hit his eyes. As he reached back and grappled with one hand for his own gun, his grip slipped with the other and he fell to the edge of the table. It tipped over and dropped him on his face on the tile, stunned. I ran over and pressed my .38 to the back of his head while I pulled his gun out of his belt and stuck it in my back pocket.

"Welcome to San Miguel," I said, kneeling on his back. "Your leader is dead. Don't make it two." He said nothing as I pulled his narrow belt free and tied it tightly around his wrists and pulled him downstairs to the second level. Keeping him covered, I unlocked the studio door. At the top of the lower staircase he swung his hip out at me to knock me off the open edge, but I saw it coming and grabbing his collar, threw him into the wall on the other side of the steps.

When we got downstairs Megan was waiting for us. Surprisingly calm, she had the gun in her hand again.

"We're OK here," I said. "There's a coil of light-weight cord in the studio, in the first cabinet on the left wall. I'd like to tie his feet too." I hadn't wanted to fumble around looking for it and try to watch him while I did it. The truth was I didn't want to kill him too if he made a move. Nathan's death was enough and this guy was only a recruit acting under orders.

Megan didn't move immediately. "Armando," she said. "I expected better of you. You've been taking orders from a corpse." He looked away, tears now flowing down his cheeks. I wasn't sure whether he was humiliated or in sudden mourning for Brother Nathan. Megan slowly mounted the steps, gripping the handrail. Stopping halfway up, she turned. "I already called Cody. He's on his way."

I made Armando lie face down next to Nathan's body while I studied the dead man's features. I hadn't had a chance to get a detailed look at him earlier.

Brother Nathan had a harsh, unfriendly face, with deep lines bracketing his mouth like parentheses. They had not relaxed even in death. His hazel eyes were wide open, vaguely staring into the clear pale sky as if looking for an inspiration that wasn't there anymore. Nathan's chin was angular and pointed, with the suggestion of a bulb at the end. His oiled black hair held no trace of gray and his nose projected aggressively over thin lips that were not quite closed. He hadn't shaved for a couple of days and his hollow cheeks were lightly bristled. I estimated his age to be early or mid fifties. If his message had been one of asceticism and vigorous discipline, his lean and taut appearance fitted that well, but I could find no trace of love or kindness in his face. The stance it offered was judgment over mercy, an Old Testament position. His followers must have been comfortable living with guilt, so perhaps Megan had been a refreshing surprise to the ones who broke away to join her.

From observing him standing with two others before Díaz' house I knew he was about five-foot-five, a lightly built man bearing a self-appointed message and a commanding manner. I took a few steps back. The closeness of death always brings a wave of sadness over me. I can never help but see myself in an unmoving figure like Nathan's. Sometimes I think this fate will catch up with me too some day, at a moment when I'm a degree or two off my game or simply coming up against someone smarter, or meaner, or more determined than I am.

But since Nathan's message allowed him to rationalize the knife murder of a young woman and her unborn child, my sympathy quickly fled. I was more neutral and indifferent to religion than Maya was, who was always militant, but there were times when I felt she got it right. Too often it ended up as an implement of control in the hands of people like Nathan.

Part of Maya's problem with the Agency was

that cases often ended like this, with one or more bodies stretched out on the ground, or going over the side into an abyss, as in our flight from Mazintla. She was lucky to have missed this round of it, since she was still out at Rancho Camarena putting Martina, her Lusitano mare, through her exercises.

At that moment Megan returned with the rope and a pair of scissors. I trussed up Armando's ankles while she opened the door for Cody, who was standing on the step outside doing his urban cop knock. She returned with her arms wrapped around him, and his around her. He was speaking softly into her ear, and as they came up the only words of his I caught were, "…now that it's over." I simply waved a welcome at him, because by that time I was already walking out to the fountain and on the phone to the police.

CHAPTER TWENTY-SEVEN

Diego Delgado of the Judicial Police arrived at our house fifteen minutes later. The two patrolmen with him were followed by Mora, the coroner, with the forensics man, and trailed by the ambulance crew a few minutes afterward.

Delgado has been our longtime contact in the police since the first case, and we've connected with him on nearly every other one. Usually it goes well. Usually. He prefers to develop his own perspective and it's not always ours. This was not the first time he'd been called to our house to investigate a death by gunshot. I led him out to the loggia and he bent over Nathan's body. He rotated the neck to look at both the entrance and exit wounds, and checked the back of the skull.

"Caught him in the crossfire today, did you, Señor Zacher? The poor little fellow didn't have a chance." He pulled a notebook out of the inside pocket of his well-worn brown suit, then pointed to the monk's cowl. "He was a religious person of some kind? Perhaps you differed over matters of faith or morals."

"You've got that right," I said, showing him the Turkish knife, which I had not touched except with the toe of my shoe, and I pointed at Megan's belly as I introduced her.

"I see. You are saying he planned to use it on her. Tell me why did you spare this other one?"

"He was already running away when I came on the scene and I don't like to shoot people in the back." With a tissue I pulled the man's gun out of my back pocket and gave it to Delgado. With his gloved hand he raised the barrel to his nose before handing it to the forensics man.

"I know you have made exceptions to that policy in the past," he said drily.

Cody came down from the upper terrace and greeted them all. We took a seat at the loggia table and told Delgado our stories in turn while the forensics man worked the scene. Megan began, detailing her background and her search for a religious cult to explore in Chiapas.

"And where did you get that small revolver?" Delgado asked her about halfway through, just as she started to get into the disappearance and presumed murder of Leo Cochrane.

"From Cody Williams, who gave it to me after he took it away from a man who was trying to kill us in

Chiapas."

Delgado nodded. "For an attractive young woman expecting a baby you are not so popular as people might imagine, yes?"

"It is true that I have been more popular in the past than I am right now. Although with these two out of circulation it might get better. I'm hopeful."

"What is your occupation?"

Megan hesitated for a moment. It was tough to answer that in a few words. Saying she was a student or recent college graduate didn't cover it adequately.

"Up until last week she was employed as the principal goddess of a religious cult in Chiapas," Cody said. "Show her some respect."

"Then she is also known by another name?"

"Jalanme'tik ta Banomil."

Delgado gave her a long look before he attempted to write this down. By now the Mazintla hairdo had relaxed to the point where Megan's hair was only aggressively wavy. She responded with a tentative smile. Cody pulled out his phone and showed him the photo he took the night we met her, with the special hair and black eye makeup.

"I see." He nodded slowly, then shrugged. "They must have different beliefs down there. Did you know the dead man?"

Without our help Megan ended the summary of

her involvement with the Mazintla cult and the death of Leo Cochrane. Cody finished by giving him the description of the red pickup with Chiapas plates. It was so like him that somehow during the chase he had managed to memorize the license number.

When we finished I pulled off our old house key from the chain I'd found in the street and gave it to him, handling it with my crime scene gloves. It would probably have the prints of either Nathan or Armando, which would prove they had tried to get in the front as well. The fact that the killing had taken place on our property where she was an invited guest was in Megan's favor, as was the fact that the assistant also had a gun and Nathan had the knife.

When Delgado left he took Megan's gun, which was illegal anyway, but said he was disinclined to file any charges on that issue since it had saved her life during a home invasion. He planned to charge Armando with breaking and entering, plus two counts of attempted murder, both of Megan and of me, since I had walked in on the crime and would've been the next victim. The fact that I had been a reliable witness many times in the past had some bearing on this outcome.

My own illegal gun was not a problem, since he had known about it for years and looked in the other direction because we needed it for the Agency. The same was true of Cody's, now prominent in his shoulder holster. Charging me with anything in the death of Nathan was not even mentioned. I could've made the case that he was already dead when my bullet passed through his neck.

We offered Diego Delgado a shooter of the good tequila as he left, but he said he had another crime scene to visit, one less urgent. I told him to come back when he wasn't so busy. Connections matter here.

By the time Maya returned from riding an hour and a half later, the body of Nathan, whose last name we had never learned, was long gone. I had tidied up the scene around the loggia and moved the teak table back into place upstairs. This was not to conceal anything from her, merely to avoid presenting her with another scene of carnage before she could put her riding gear away. The powdery plaster debris was swept up at the base of the parapet, although I hadn't filled the bullet hole yet. I was making fajitas for lunch for all of us. At Megan's request, when I went to get the chicken breast and vegetables, I also picked up a *tres leches* cake at the Mega supermarket to celebrate the successful outcome of the case. Cody guarded her carefully in my absence.

Later that week, when I was wrapping up the paperwork and final report on this case, my first instinct was to label the file *The Return of Jalanme'tik ta Banomil*, but Maya vetoed this. No one could pronounce it correctly anyway, she said, even Megan, so we decided to file it simply as *Lost in Chiapas*.

CHAPTER TWENTY-EIGHT

The demise of Brother Nathan not only allowed us to finally put an end to the case mentally, but also freed Megan to look for a place of her own to live. Maya threw herself into helping her do this with in an almost indecent gusto, pleading that she knew the neighborhoods better than any of us. Within twenty-four hours they found a studio apartment down the hill in the nearby Guadiana neighborhood and signed a year's lease. It was located in a locked compound of five other units, and offered an easy walk downtown. Maya also got Megan hooked up with a doctor who had a large obstetrics clientele, and this woman also worked in other areas, notably as a nutritionist. This town isn't big enough to support any strictly specialized practices. Most pregnant women in the campo use midwives, or even simply family members for help in childbirth.

We had notified the Andersons briefly on our return home that Megan was safe and traveling with us, saying a more complete report would follow. My next

Agency project following the death of Brother Nathan and Megan getting settled was to frame a note to the Andersons that gently explained why we would be leaving it to her to decide how she would next contact them, as well as to sketch in the outlines of the case as it progressed. I'm always reluctant to lay out for the client the full degree of risk we take on, so I prefer to leave the process a little vague. For example, I would've described our flight from Mazintla simply as "using improvised transportation," if I had wanted to get into that degree of detail. I don't know whether any of our clients have ever realized that we've killed people in their behalf. Perhaps one or two have figured it out.

Maya had drawn up a document that detailed our time and expenses, and it came out that the Andersons only owed us an additional $1145. The nine thousand they'd already paid covered the rest, including the guide fee for Artemio Díaz and the deductible on my vehicle damage. I have to say that it now looks nearly as good as new, although not quite. You never get a stolen vehicle back just the way it was, and if it had not been vital to our return home, I would've prayed that we never saw it again.

My conversation with Megan about redemption and forgiveness never left my mind as we worked on this message, although I'd said nothing more about it to Maya and nothing at all to Cody. His focus was always on evidence and risk, elements that exist far closer to the ground. Here's what I came up with after several drafts that all four of us batted around vigorously before we settled on it:

Dear Mr. & Mrs. Anderson,

As you know from our earlier message containing a photo of Megan with Paul and me, we located her in an obscure mountain village in Chiapas called Mazintla. There she was serving as an interim pastor for a small congregation that had recently broken off from a larger faction. We soon discovered that Leo Cochrane had been killed by unknown persons from that original group, and we immediately decided that Megan was at considerable risk in her circumstances. She was living alone. Because this area was part of the Zapatista territory, there was little organized law enforcement. While Megan had several amateur bodyguards, she no longer felt she could leave the grounds of her church in safety.

At this point we intervened and made a strong case to her that she should leave with us and go at least as far as San Cristobal de las Casas. Reluctantly she agreed, but we soon discovered the other side had followed us. Our vehicle was stolen and damaged in this process.

After a difficult road trip, we ultimately brought her with us safely to San Miguel de Allende. Although she survived the experience uninjured, in her current upset state of mind she is uncertain whether she wishes to be in contact with you immediately, or anyone from the States right now, and so we have respected her desires and she will determine when she plans to resume communication with you. Naturally this is not the outcome we would've preferred, but she is of age and the decision is hers to make. She is living comfortably in a secure location in a gated compound. Although we believe that none of her pursuers have followed her here, we will continue to stay in touch with her on a regular basis.

We are grateful that you chose the Paul Zacher Agency for this sensitive task, and we believe we have accomplished your fundamental goal in a most satisfactory manner.

The final billing and expense breakdown is attached.

Best Wishes,

Maya Sanchez, President.

This is the message I ultimately finished for Maya's signature when she said she preferred not to do it herself, pleading a lack of objectivity on this case. It addressed every objection raised by Cody and Megan. We were all eager to bring up nothing about the circumstances of Brother Nathan's death. After all, the risk was now finished, so why alarm the Andersons any further?

While most of our client communications are confidential, I have included it in these notes because Garrett Anderson released his response more publicly. I will therefore post his comments too, since he also copied Diego Delgado, and I no longer consider any of this exchange to be private. Anderson's email wonderfully illustrates how poorly clients sometimes grasp the difficulty of field operations.

(No salutation)

If ever there was a poorer excuse for a detective shop than the Paul Zacher Agency I would like to hear about it. You ought to try some other way to earn a living because your sorry efforts have only resulted in making a difficult family situation worse. Hiding behind Maya's signature is only a pathetic ruse. You should've written it yourself, like a man. And don't think you ought to go back to painting, either. I've seen better stuff in a fifth grade art class than what's hanging on your walls. It's no surprise that you don't even bother to frame most of it. Don't ever expect a recommendation from us; in fact my next note is going to go to the Better Business Bureau with a copy to the police in San Miguel. I can see now why you live in México, because you sure as hell could never make a living here in the States where ability counts for something.

You can kiss that additional $1145 goodbye because you're not getting one more cent from us. Go ahead and sue me, asshole.

Sincerely yours,

Garrett and Zina Anderson

Well, as they say, not everyone had an equally good time of it in this case, but some of our outings are like that. I do admit, that although she was not the one who hired us, Megan Anderson ended up being the client. Had she found a need to evaluate the performance of the Paul Zacher Agency, I'm sure her judgment would've come out differently than her father's. In some ways I thought we might have witnessed a coming of age for her. Sometimes it all awakens in a rush when the obstacles, in this case Garrett Anderson and the late Brother Nathan, are removed. She must have felt she had found a non-controlling stepfather in Cody, who was genuinely devoted to her best interest.

Garrett Anderson and the cult leader Brother Nathan were not the only ones in this case to come up with less than they wished for. The poor people of Mazintla, torn between two cults, ended up with no religious establishment left in their town. If neither belief system had supplied them with a viable theology, one at least had provided an aura of kindness and benevolence, if only briefly. The disappearance of both meant an end of hope, the most valuable aspect of either. I tried not to speculate on what might appear to replace them. It was not an optimistic train of thought, and at this point in any case I am always eager to move on.

A few weeks passed, filled with an unsurprising eruption of painting for me, and a vivid focus on riding for Maya. Martina was genuinely happy to have her back in the saddle again. After the holidays, and in the later days of her pregnancy we sometimes saw Megan with Cody as they walked arm-in-arm in the *jardín*, our central plaza. They had clearly grown closer in ways neither of them could have imagined. Maya and I decided we couldn't define their relationship any better than saying they had both found more than one important element in it that was missing from their lives before they met. I only know that Cody never told her what to do, but always supported her decisions. If she ever needed to ask for any advice, he certainly would've been the man to turn to.

Three months to the day since we first encountered Megan emerging from the old church in Mazintla wearing her gauzy skirt and palm fiber breastplates, she went into labor. After fourteen hours she gave birth to a strapping boy who weighed nine pounds and two ounces. We were told he greeted the world with a roar. She named him Cody Anderson on that last day of February in the new year.

Our partner in crime solving had never been a parent, but Cody Williams embraced his promotion to grandfather as if he'd been waiting offstage his entire life for precisely this cue.

The lesson Megan had learned in her sixty-day reign as the cult leader and local goddess named Jalanme'tik ta Banomil, one she had quoted to us the night we met her, had now become her mantra in life, but it was not drawn from theology or morality. We had come into the hospital room to see the infant Cody and his mother, once both were cleaned up, and her face was glowing. The elder Cody was holding the child, rocking him back and forth as he walked past the window with a long view over our town.

"You can't fake this, you know?" Megan said with the broadest of smiles. "It needs to be the real thing." She added that once little Cody was settled into his new world, she thought they would be getting more engaged and joining one of the privately funded charitable groups in San Miguel, one specializing in prenatal care and midwifery for country women. Perhaps she could set up a small daycare unit for those mothers-to-be to use while they were being attended to by the medical staff.

She realized it was a humble task, but one she now understood could have the highest value for women without partners, which is often the case here. Many husbands and lovers had gone over the border to find work, and helping their families in their absence required dedication more than parlor tricks or magic skills. Little Cody could be the permanent greeter for newcomers his own age. With his new grandfather in attendance, and especially with a mother with broad experience in matters of growth and survival, we all felt confident of the infant being launched on the right path.

I didn't suggest it, but I thought that might be a more realistic continuation of the mission Megan had discovered in Mazintla during her goddess period, one based on kindness and support for people who didn't have many options or prospects. Big Cody would be taking her around to look at the different facilities and programs when she felt she was ready.

"I can't believe that after all the bloody work I did today, I'm still so fat," she said, as we were about to leave her hospital room. "I'll never be a goddess again. That phase of my life is over."

Maya agreed, nodding in ardent support of this idea. "Nothing lasts forever," she said, sympathetically.

Cody came over to Megan and placed the sleepy infant in her arms. I was sorry I'd forgotten my camera, and Maya and I often left our cells at home when we weren't on a case. Going out the door, the last thing we saw was Megan raising her hand to caress Cody's jowls as he bent over to kiss her forehead. I swear I saw them shrink in size by a little at her touch. It was nice to think we were all mutually supportive even if we didn't always understand how it worked.

Maya and I came home later that afternoon to celebrate with a couple of margaritas. This kind of finish was a long Agency tradition, dating in fact from our first outing, to review our process and celebrate the end of a case. We had always included Cody before, but this time he was otherwise engaged on a family matter. Although this case had seemed to finish a while back, right after the demise of Brother Nathan, the birth of Cody Anderson was received as the triumph it was, a beginning wrapped in an ending, so it had a special significance for all of us. In a sense, little Cody had been with us through the entire journey.

I assembled the margaritas and brought them out to the edge of the garden. Orlando, our long-tailed staff grackle, approached to see whether I had provided any fried pork skins for him. As usual, I had. It was the finish of a fruitful and rewarding day.

Maya and I were both tired and looking forward to tomorrow as a new start. We had both unconsciously wondered whether little Cody would make it through without blemish. I kissed her and held her closely for a long healing moment before we sat down. This was the occasion when she enjoyed being able to say that no one had died this time, whenever that was possible. Mostly, as with this case, it was not.

For coasters out on the plank table in the loggia, we now had Megan's two woven palm fiber breastplates. The string link between them had been trimmed away, along with the chain loop for her neck and the cords that secured them behind her back. I had asked Megan, as I sometimes do with a client, if she would give us a souvenir of the case, and after a little thought, she said I might relish having these, since I had appeared to enjoy them so much when she wore them that first night in Mazintla, in my search, as she reminded me, for a *bruja*.

Nothing goes to waste here in México.